## She knew he was just as uneasy about being in bed with her as she was

Maybe it was because he knew he'd fraudulently vowed to love, honor and cherish her. In her own heart, the vows had truly been made. Tonight she felt like a wife in bed with her new husband.

She turned on her side and regarded the pillows that separated them.

Common sense told her this was no time to give up the dubious honor of being the last twenty-nine-year-old virgin in Greece and, maybe, in the United States.

Her conscience reminded her that the marriage was only a charade for the benefit of the United States immigration authorities.

But desire told her that, after all, they *were* married. She wondered how it would feel to share the longing inside for someone of her own to love and to cherish. To honor the vows she'd made to Adam...

# MY BIG FAKE GREEN-CARD WEDDING

## Mollie Molay

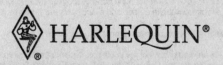

# HARLEQUIN®

TORONTO • NEW YORK • LONDON
AMSTERDAM • PARIS • SYDNEY • HAMBURG
STOCKHOLM • ATHENS • TOKYO • MILAN • MADRID
PRAGUE • WARSAW • BUDAPEST • AUCKLAND

In memory of my late husband, Louis Matza,
and our own hilarious wedding, where our two cultures
managed to maintain an uneasy peace.

And to our two wonderful daughters,
Elaine Fox and Joy Steinhardt.
Love you lots,
Mom

ISBN 0-373-16987-6

MY BIG FAKE GREEN-CARD WEDDING

Copyright © 2003 by Mollie Molé.

## ABOUT THE AUTHOR

After working for a number of years as a logistics contract administrator in the aircraft industry, Mollie Molay turned to a career she found far more satisfying—writing romance novels. Mollie lives in Northridge, California, surrounded by her two daughters and eight grandchildren, many of whom find their way into her books. She enjoys hearing from her readers and welcomes comments. You can write to her at Harlequin Books, 225 Duncan Mill Road, Don Mills, Ontario, Canada M3B 3K9.

## Books by Mollie Molay

### HARLEQUIN AMERICAN ROMANCE
560—FROM DRIFTER TO DADDY
597—HER TWO HUSBANDS
616—MARRIAGE BY MISTAKE
638—LIKE FATHER, LIKE SON
682—NANNY & THE BODYGUARD
703—OVERNIGHT WIFE
729—WANTED: DADDY
776—FATHER IN TRAINING
799—DADDY BY CHRISTMAS
815—MARRIED BY MIDNIGHT
839—THE GROOM CAME C.O.D.
879—BACHELOR-AUCTION BRIDEGROOM
897—THE BABY IN THE BACK SEAT
938—THE DUCHESS & HER BODYGUARD*
947—SECRET SERVICE DAD*
954—COMMANDER'S LITTLE SURPRISE*
987—MY BIG FAKE GREEN-CARD WEDDING

*Grooms in Uniform

Don't miss any of our special offers. Write to us at the following address for information on our newest releases.

Harlequin Reader Service
U.S.: 3010 Walden Ave., P.O. Box 1325, Buffalo, NY 14269
Canadian: P.O. Box 609, Fort Erie, Ont. L2A 5X3

# KOURABIETHES
### (Greek Butter Cookies)

1 cup unsalted butter
1/2 tsp baking powder
1 egg yolk
1 cup confectioner's sugar, stirred
1 tbsp brandy
3 cups flour (approx.)
Walnuts or almonds (optional)
1 lb confectioner's sugar to sift onto cookies as soon as they come out of the oven

Mix butter and sugar until very light and fluffy. Stir in egg yolk and brandy.

Mix flour and baking powder. Add to butter mixture with sifted confectioner's sugar, a little at a time. Knead well until dough is smooth. If too soft, add a little flour. Add nuts, if desired.

Take small pieces of dough and shape into little balls or into crescents. Place on lightly greased baking sheets. Bake in moderate oven (350° F) for approximately 20 minutes.

Roll cookies in additional confectioner's sugar while warm. Sift more confectioner's sugar over cookies to keep well coated to keep moist.

Makes about 3 1/2 dozen cookies.

# Chapter One

*U.S. Embassy*
*Athens, Greece*

"You are almost thirty years old, daughter. It's time you found yourself a husband! If you don't, I will find one for you!"

With her father's voice echoing in her ears, Melina Kostos hung up the phone. Today wasn't her lucky day, she thought as she stared at the run in her smoky-gray nylons. The notice advising her that her position as the U.S. embassy's bilingual receptionist was about to be downsized wasn't helping. Without a job, she no longer had a reason to argue away her father's concern over her single status.

How could she tell her father that she didn't want a husband? At least, not yet. Or that she had no intention of being Athens's last virgin over the age of 29 if she could help it? She not only had some living to do, but no part of that plan included letting a man control her life.

What she most wanted was a green card that would allow her to go to the United States to work. The past two years at the U.S. embassy had left her with a keen interest in the country. At least there, women seemed to be free.

If only she had someone to talk to besides the two close friends she roomed with. Eleni and Arianna, who worked at the embassy with her, were also Greek natives and, in one way at least, in the same position she was: single. She wasn't sure even they would understand the way she felt.

It would be difficult to expect anyone not from a traditional Greek family like hers to understand her father's call, she mused as she stared at the telephone. Sure, she was almost thirty and, for all intents and purposes, on her own. Unfortunately, her age was not about to stop her father from demanding she marry and raise a family. As the only daughter in an old-fashioned Greek family, her father's voice was still the law.

She was unhappily envisioning the kind of suitor her father had in mind when a burst of laughter caught her attention.

"We're going up to the roof garden for lunch, Melina. Want to come with us? Melina, are you listening to me?"

Startled out of her reverie, Melina managed to smile brightly. Arianna and Eleni waited in front of her desk for her reply. "Yes, of course," Melina answered. "I was lost in thought."

"About what?"

She gestured to the termination notice. "I just received notice my position is being joined with Anna's. Actually," she added wistfully, "I was thinking how wonderful it would be if I could get a green card and go to the United States. I would like to work there for a few years before I settle down." She went on to tell them about her father's threatening phone call.

Arianna clucked her dismay. "There must be someone here at the embassy who could help you!"

Melina shook her head. "I don't know anyone here well enough to ask. I'm not even sure if it would be legal, anyway."

Arianna rubbed her stomach. "Well, come on. We can talk about it over lunch. I'm hungry."

"Go on ahead." Melina smiled at her pleasantly plump friend who loved the rich Greek food the embassy served. "I'll lock my desk and meet you at the elevator."

Melina set the telephone button that would route incoming calls to Anna and fumbled in her bag for her vanity case to freshen up.

Would the woman who stared back at her in the

small mirror ever be free of the controlling influence of a man? Her younger two brothers had somehow managed to find their own way without her father's unwelcome influence. Why couldn't she?

*Because you are a woman in an established society,* a small pragmatic voice answered. In a traditional country like Greece, unmarried women were still expected to be guided by their fathers. Especially in her home village of Nafplion.

Not me! Melina vowed as she made for the elevator. Somewhere, somehow, she would find a way to keep her independence and to live out her heart's desire. At least for a few years.

"Ah, Melina, there you are! I was just coming back to get you." Eleni pushed her way through the open door. "Hurry, the elevator will leave without you."

"There's always another elevator." Melina laughed as she squeezed in alongside her friend. "What's so special about this one?"

"Trust me." Eleni wiggled her way to the back of the elevator and pulled Melina with her. "This one *is* our elevator."

"I'm starving." Arianna wiggled and grumbled beside her. "It's so crowded in here, I can hardly breathe."

Pushed back against a solid, masculine body, Melina quickly realized she was almost skin to skin with the man who stood behind her. "Excuse me," she murmured, and tried to give him space. It didn't work. What *was* working, to her dismay, was the effect of the man's pungent shaving lotion. The scent, combined with the pressure of his firm chest against her back, brought her hormones to attention. The sound of his deep, raspy voice in her ear didn't help her to think too rationally, either.

Wondering if the intimate contact was having the same effect on him, she belatedly realized that he was speaking with an American accent. Ignoring her faint apology, he continued his conversation with the other man who also shared their space.

"My ex called this morning to inform me she intends to remarry next week."

"Congratulations!" a Greek-accented voice answered. "Just think of all the money in alimony you'll save."

"That's not the point, Peter," the American went on. "Jeanette made it clear she expects me to come home to take care of little Jamie while she's on her honeymoon."

"That is understandable, my friend. After all, Jamie is your daughter."

"Of course. I'm nuts about Jamie," the American agreed. "It's not just the short notice, I don't know how to take care of a little girl on a daily basis."

Melina felt like an eavesdropper as the very masculine and warm chest behind her heaved a deep sigh. "The problem is, I have to travel on business a great deal," the American went on. "I'm going to have to look for both a housekeeper and a nanny when I get back to the States."

"Why spend money for two women when one would do?"

"One?" There was a pause. "I'm not sure one woman could handle both jobs. You have a family, Pete. Which do you think is a better idea, a housekeeper or a nanny?"

"Neither," Pete answered with a wry laugh. "We Greeks are more practical than you Americans. Forget a nanny or a housekeeper. What you need is a wife."

Melina's antenna quivered as the elevator stopped one more time to let a passenger out before continuing on up to the roof. Myriad thoughts raced through Melina's mind.

A housekeeper? The position had to be, as her American colleagues frequently said, a piece of cake. As a dutiful Greek daughter, she was well versed in taking care of a home.... She'd learned to cook for five people... How difficult could feeding two people be?

A nanny? As the only girl in her family, she'd often helped her mother with the care of her two younger brothers. For the past two years she'd also taught Greek language to young embassy children and, in the process, had wiped more than a few runny noses. How different could the job of a nanny to one child be?

Here was her chance to get her heart's desire and still be able to put off her father's demand that she marry, she thought. It was worth a try.

The elevator, empty except for Melina, her two friends and the two men behind her, finally reached the roof garden. Tables, shaded against the afternoon sun by dark green umbrellas, were surrounded by pots of colorful flowers and vine-covered trellises. The scent of warm food at the buffet table filled the air.

Eleni poked her in the ribs. "We're here," she whispered. "Go ahead. Now is your chance."

Her chance? Had Eleni overheard the men's conversation and put one and one together? Had Eleni read her mind?

Melina was so engrossed in preparing a logical approach to the American that one of the two men exiting the elevator bumped into her.

"Ah, Melina Kostos! I thought that was you!"

Melina pulled her wayward thoughts together. "Uh, hello, Peter. I'm sorry, I wasn't looking. How are you?"

"Excellent," he said with a broad smile. "Even better now that I've met you again. Come, let me introduce you to my American friend, Adam Blake.''

Peter Stakis was a friendly sort and a member of the Greek embassy's trade office. Peter often visited the American embassy on business. He was also a good friend of her family's. ''I am pleased to meet you, Mr. Blake.''

''Likewise,'' the American businessman said, an admiring look in his eyes.

To Melina's relief he looked approachable. She decided to come right out with it. To talk to him frankly and to solicit his cooperation. It was just a matter of finding the right way to say what she wanted to say without appearing the complete fool.

She was about to introduce her friends when Eleni grabbed Arianna's arm and made for an empty table. ''We'll see you later!''

Peter raised an eyebrow at their abrupt departure, shrugged, and gestured to the buffet table offering up hot food, salads, sandwiches and drinks. ''Since it appears you are now alone, will you join us for lunch, Melina?''

''Thank you, I would like to.'' Melina couldn't figure out how Eleni had known which elevator to take for Melina to meet her destiny, but she was grateful. Even more so when Eleni had had the foresight to take Arianna and leave. Now, to find a way to get rid of Peter before she made her pitch. The fewer people who overheard her, the better. Especially someone who knew her family.

The scents of pita-wrapped sandwiches and the traditional Greek-salad of cucumbers, walnuts and tomatoes pulled her to the buffet table. Maybe, she prayed silently, her stomach would stop fluttering if it were full.

"Salad, please," she told the server. "With just a bit of oil and vinegar dressing."

"Is that all you're going to eat?" the American asked as he hovered over a tray of moussaka.

Melina glanced at the inviting displays of cold cucumber pita sandwiches and the container of hot moussaka. Never mind the chocolate chip cookies and the baklava that begged for her attention. It all looked delicious. But the truth was, she was too nervous to eat. It wasn't every day a woman came face-to-face with her destiny.

"I usually don't eat much at noon," she answered, gesturing for a glass of iced tea.

Peter's American friend didn't seem to have a problem with food, she thought enviously as she watched him ask for a double helping of moussaka. Like all Greek girls, she'd been raised to know how to cook for a family. If she wound up as Adam Blake's housekeeper, she vowed, he would never lack the Greek food he seemed to favor.

"How are your parents, your brothers, Melina?" Peter asked as they were seated.

"Fine, thank you," she said, sipping her iced tea to take her mind off Adam Blake's clear hazel eyes, the deep cleft in his square jaw and his innate sensuality. How in heaven's name could she be attracted to a man she'd just noticed but had never been introduced to before? "Busy with the family pistachio business."

"Good, good. You have a fine family, Melina. I shall have to visit them soon and pay my respects to your father." Melina blinked and hoped the visit wouldn't take place too soon.

She gathered enough information during lunch to learn that Adam Blake was a U.S. importer of such Greek products as extra-virgin olive oil and fine wines. Which meant, unfortunately, that he traveled a great deal. It was no wonder that he was dismayed at having to take over the care of his little daughter.

Just as well, Melina thought, that he wasn't going to be around every day or she'd be a basket case. She caught him eyeing the way she nervously played with the top button on her blouse. Though she tried to return his gaze casually, she couldn't seem to keep her fingers still under his stare. To add to her problem, his blatant masculinity sent her mind down paths a woman who wanted to apply for the job as his housekeeper had no right to tread. She had to approach the man with a business proposition—no more, no less.

It wasn't until the men were into their dessert that Melina had gathered enough courage to speak her mind. The honeyed scent of the slice of baklava pastry wafted across the table.

She took a deep breath. "I hope you don't mind, Mr. Blake, but I overheard you in the elevator telling Peter you are looking for someone to help you take care of your young daughter."

"Why yes, I guess I am." Adam looked at her with growing interest. "Why, do you know someone who might be interested?"

Melina wiped her dry lips with her paper napkin. "Yes, I do. Me."

Adam Blake looked as if she'd hit him right between the eyes with a brick. Compared to the train that suddenly seemed to roar through her already queasy stomach, it was a mild reaction. "You?"

"Yes, me," she repeated firmly, and took another deep swallow of iced tea.

"Why?" Adam frowned and glanced around the patio. "I thought you worked here at the embassy."

"I do, for now. Actually, my position is being eliminated—for financial reasons."

"You want a position as a housekeeper?" Adam Blake repeated cautiously. "That would be quite a change for you, wouldn't it?"

"Perhaps," Melina answered quietly, trying to still the inner voice that was cautioning her to go slowly. "I have my reasons."

Adam Blake regarded her for a long moment. From the way she kept playing with the button on her blouse, she knew it was obvious that she was nervous. He finally asked, "And those reasons are?"

Melina glanced at Peter Stakis before she answered. Something in her eyes must have told him she wanted privacy. He rose and pushed back his chair. "Nice to see you again, Melina. Please say hello to your father for me. Adam, I'll see you downstairs in the trade office when you're through with lunch."

WITH PETER GONE, Adam sat back in his chair and stared, fascinated by the play of her finely shaped fingers against her slender throat. Uneasily, he prepared to listen to Melina. He didn't know her, or anything about her other than what he'd gleaned during lunch. She was beautiful in the classic Greek way—dark hair, almond-shaped, lavender-colored eyes, slender and tall. She was obviously intelligent or she wouldn't have been employed as the embassy's receptionist.

Peter had sent his regards to her parents and her brothers, he mused, so he knew she came from a

well-regarded family. But as a housekeeper? Did he
dare take a chance?

"Go ahead," he said, not convinced, but willing
to listen. "I'm all ears."

She glanced at his ears and looked bewildered.
Until he laughed and explained. "It's an old American expression," he said. "I meant, you have my
full attention. Why would you want to help take care
of my daughter instead of remaining here in
Greece?"

"I will take care of your little girl," she said
slowly before visibly taking another deep breath and
plunging on, "in exchange for a green card that will
enable me to stay and work in your country later."

Adam blinked. It hadn't occurred to him he could
be her ticket to the United States. To add to his
dilemma, green cards were becoming increasingly
difficult to obtain. Melina's offer, though not exactly
conventional, was worthy of consideration if she
was as authentic as she seemed. After all, he needed
her. Or, at least, someone like her.

On the other hand, he only had her word that she
was being let go for economic reasons. Maybe all
she had was ambition and a taste for wanderlust.
How long would she remain with him as his housekeeper or as his daughter's nanny once she got her
hands on that green card? Was she worth the risk?

The more he thought about Melina's proposition

the more leery he became of the idea of bringing a desirable but virtual stranger into his home.

Adam gazed into her earnest lavender eyes and finally made her an offer no woman in her right mind would accept.

"I don't need a housekeeper or a nanny," he said as he remembered Peter's frank comment. He intended to politely lay his cards on the table for an alternate proposition. A proposition she was bound to turn down and that would afford him a graceful exit. "What I really need is a wife."

Her eyes narrowed, a blush covered her finely etched cheeks. She froze.

"A wife?" The words were hardly a whisper.

"Yes, a wife," he answered. He sat back, waiting for her to tell him he was out of his mind and to leave. The fine hairs on the back of his neck started to tingle at the speculative look that slowly came into her eyes. Maybe he hadn't made himself clear enough. "You know, the kind who says 'I do' in front of a preacher," he said, mentally crossing his fingers.

"And a green card?"

"You got it. It's all or nothing."

Melina hesitated while she silently tallied the factors in Adam Blake's favor.

He wasn't exactly a stranger to her. A respected

businessman, she'd seen him come and go through the embassy for the past two years.

His aura whenever she'd caught a glimpse of him, until today, had been clearly businesslike and above reproach.

He also appeared to be a close friend of Peter's. That alone was enough to persuade her.

Her inner voice cautioned her to go slowly. Why was he offering to marry a woman he didn't know instead of hiring her on as a housekeeper or nanny?

"How much of a wife did you have in mind?" she asked cautiously.

Adam blinked. He hadn't thought that far, nor had he thought that she would accept his ridiculous proposition. All he *had* thought about was a way to get rid of her by suggesting the impossible. Now what would he do if she were truly serious about taking him up on his off-the-wall alternative?

And why had he listened to Peter, anyway?

He shot Melina a suggestive smile deliberately calculated to change her mind and to get them both off the hook. "Let's just say it wouldn't only be a marriage of convenience."

Melina regarded him warily and rapidly considered her options. Reared to marry young, to have children and to raise a family, she was within a heartbeat of achieving her heart's desire of going to the United States. Most women would jump at the chance to marry a man like Adam Blake instead of entering an arranged marriage. At least Adam was handsome, successful and an attentive father.

Would she come to love him? That was another story. She didn't know him well enough to judge. Still, he had to be better than what awaited her at home. And wasn't a marriage of convenience what her father had actually had in mind when he'd told her he would find a husband for her if she didn't find one for herself?

Was there any difference between a stranger her father might choose for her and a man she chose for herself? she mused as she regarded Adam. Marriage and children *had* been her ultimate goal, hadn't it?

Her body tingled at the thought. She had a few reservations, but she couldn't bring herself to turn back. She held out her hand. ''As they say in your country, Adam Blake, it's a deal.''

Adam swallowed the lump in his throat. Desperate times called for desperate measures, he thought wildly, or he was going to wind up a married man again. He *had* to give Melina a few things to think about before the situation got out of hand. For sure, he couldn't afford to encourage her by taking her outstretched hand. Or to tease himself. Not when he knew he had to come clean or never be able to live with himself.

''Miss Kostos,'' he said after he took a deep

breath. "I have to be honest with you. I'm afraid I was out of line when I said I needed a wife. My offer was impulsive, and, now that it's out in the open, incredibly stupid. The truth is, I don't *really* want a wife. I've been married before and I wasn't a good husband, or so I was told. However, I do need a housekeeper or a nanny. And I do need to get one as soon as possible."

Melina regarded him thoughtfully. Still, if he was that honest with her, she had to be honest with him. "That's too bad, because I think I need a husband."

"You think?" A cautious look came into his eyes.

"Well, yes," she said with a wry smile, "but it's not what you think. I meant it when I said I wanted to go to America and to get a green card to work there. The only way I know how to get the card is to find a sponsor and to apply through the proper channels. That might take forever." She sighed. "Or—" she looked at him in a way that made his heart race "—I could marry an American citizen and *then* apply for a card. I think that would be easier. Of course," she added, afraid he might think she was mercenary. "I promise I will…what you Americans say, pay my way by taking care of your home and your daughter."

Adam's mind boggled at the thought she still

wanted to be his wife even after he'd confessed he wasn't good husband material. "Just like that?"

"Yes, just like that," she agreed. "As for my qualifications, you should know I am the oldest child in my family, with two younger brothers. If you knew my brothers, God bless them both, you would know I am well qualified to care for a little girl. As for taking care of you—" she blushed at the possible interpretation of her words and pushed forward "—I have been well trained in keeping a home."

Adam felt bewildered...until he realized the scheme she was suggesting might work. If he didn't want a real wife, she obviously didn't want a real husband. She wanted a green card and a chance to see his country. A marriage certificate would, in the long run, get them both what they wanted.

"Okay. It's a deal. Of course," he went on, "you should realize we have to make things look legitimate or the immigration authorities at home will never buy our sudden marriage."

Melina's gaze turned wary. "What do you have in mind to make the marriage look real?"

"We'll have to look as if we fell in love at first sight and couldn't wait to get married," he said with a hint of laughter in his voice and a twinkle in his eyes. "I'll even get in touch with Peter and ask him to back us up. From what I know about him, he's a real romantic. By the time I get through, he's bound to believe I fell for you like a ton of bricks. Of course, the real reason for the marriage will have to remain between us. How does that sound?''

It was the twinkle in his eyes and the beguiling crooked smile on his lips that gave Melina pause. If Adam had been attractive and sexy when he was serious, he was even more so when he poked fun at himself. Too bad they hadn't had time to really get to know each other, she thought wistfully. Adam Blake was the type of man she would have liked to have for a real husband.

''What did you have in mind to show we have a real marriage?'' she finally asked.

''Easy. We'll get married and go on a honeymoon. How does a weekend in Corfu sound to you?''

# Chapter Two

Melina blushed. She'd agreed to go through the motions of getting married, but a honeymoon? He was talking about pretending to share the ultimate intimate interlude when they hardly knew each other! Of course, it was true that she could hardly control her attraction to him. Was it his broad shoulders, the laughter in his eyes or the strong reach of his hands set alongside hers on the table? Whatever the attraction, it was working. "A honeymoon? You're joking, aren't you?"

"No," he said with a quirked eyebrow. "That's what people do when they get married."

Melina wasn't sure she was comfortable with the way he was looking at her. The expression in his eyes made her feel as if he were actually imagining her in their marriage bed on their wedding night. The picture was so vivid, she instinctively warmed at the thought of his arms around her, the taste of his full, masculine lips on hers. Of heated skin gliding over heated skin and her hands running through his thick sandy-brown hair.

What might happen next if she wasn't careful, was what bothered her. As a virgin, she could only imagine such a scenario.

Another woman might have been overwhelmed by the anticipatory gleam in Adam's eyes, but Melina was too intelligent to believe what she saw there was real. Nevertheless, she had to admit that he was wonderfully sexy.

At the moment she felt as if he was savoring her as a cat savored cream—or was it a canary? No matter how hard she tried, she couldn't keep all those odd American expressions straight. But considering this was only a game they had agreed to play, he looked entirely too pleased with himself.

"Since this is going to be a marriage of convenience," she said firmly, "we have to make a few rules."

"Rules?" Adam looked taken aback at her request, but she didn't care. He'd laid out his thoughts about their so-called marriage. It was her turn.

"Yes, rules. Agreed?"

Adam smiled. "Sure, but remember, this has to look like a real marriage."

The more Adam appeared to be amused, the more Melina became determined to set limits. This wasn't going to be a love-'em-and-leave-'em relationship she'd seen in too many American movies. She intended that they would appear loving without becoming lovers.

"Actually, I have only two requests," she said. "The first one is 'no touching in private.'"

Adam's eyebrows rose. She could just imagine what he was thinking. "If this is a game, you have to remember all games have some rules."

"Okay, but remember, we're supposed to be in love."

"In public perhaps," she agreed reluctantly. "In private, no." The no-touching rule was important to her. Not because of what Adam might do, but because she couldn't trust herself not to go up in flames if he did touch her.

"That's all?" he asked with an amused grin that made her toes tingle.

"No." She ignored his crooked smile. He might think their proposed arrangement was amusing, but she was serious. "If we're going to make this look real, you have to meet my father and mother."

The smile on Adam's face disappeared. "I suppose I could do that. Anything more? Better get it all off your chest now, I wouldn't want any surprises."

Chest! Melina blushed at the unintentional reference to her breasts. If he kept this up, she would have to make up a few more rules to help her keep her distance.

"I can't think of another rule right now," she said, "but I'm sure I'll have a few more as we go along."

Adam shrugged. "All right. Just give me some advance notice when you do. So, are you sure about my having to meet your father?"

"Yes. I don't know how they do it in your country, but in Greece a woman's intended husband asks her father for permission to marry her."

Melina's stomach roiled as she pictured the look on her father's face when she brought home an American. How would he react when she announced she was about to marry him?

Her father had made it clear from the time she'd entered her teens that the only man worthy of becoming his son-in-law was a Greek man, preferably from their village. The man would have to be old and wise enough to care for her. Just as her father had taken care of her mother, she could hear her father say. Privately, Melina knew just who had taken care of whom.

Since Melina had watched her mother raise three children, run a household, help with the family pistachio business and satisfy her husband, she knew better.

"You need your father's approval before you

marry?'' Adam asked, sounding surprised. ''You *are* over twenty-one aren't you?''

Clearly the man didn't understand Greek culture. Stung, Melina defended herself and her family's dearly held tradition—even if she found it confining. ''I am old enough. In the first place, twenty-first century or not, most Greek women are brought up to believe that their father as well as their priest speaks for God. In the second place, you did say we have to make our bargain look good. That includes meeting my father.''

Adam had the grace to blush.

''You also need to know my parents live in Naf-plion, a small village outside of Athens. They are, what we call in Greek, *horiatees,* people who come from small villages. I suppose you could say they're not very modern in their thinking.''

Melina's gaze locked with Adam's as she spoke. She knew without being told that something more than her traditional upbringing was bothering him. Maybe it wasn't every day a man proposed marriage, but he'd been married before and thus had to have proposed to a woman at least once.

''I don't need my father's consent,'' she went on, ''but he has waited a long time to see me married. I owe him my respect. I can't possibly marry you without at least introducing you. I also have to ask

my mother to plan the wedding. It's a family tradition.''

To her surprise, Adam suddenly choked on his
last bite of baklava. She rounded the table in seconds
and pounded him on his back. What could she have
said that could have caused such a reaction? ''Are
you all right?''

''Er, I think so.'' Adam reached for her iced tea,
the only liquid on the table, took a deep swallow
and cleared his throat. ''We don't have time to *plan*
a wedding. I have to be back in the States early next
week to pick up my daughter, Jamie.''

Disappointed, Melina gave up her childhood
dream of a church wedding, of wearing her mother's
wedding gown and of her father walking her down
the aisle. She consoled herself that at the moment
her more pressing need was to get that green card.
''I'll talk it over with my mother…maybe she can
talk to the priest and arrange for a small church wedding.''

''No time,'' he said firmly. ''We barely have time
for a weekend honeymoon. I have to be home next
Wednesday for Jamie.''

Melina sighed wistfully. ''Your home is the
United States. My home is here. That is, for now.
It's not easy to give up all of the traditions I grew
up with. They are all I know.''

Melina watched mixed emotions pass over Adam's

face. Most women would have thought his plan to marry her just after meeting her was romantic, her friend Eleni With the Sixth Sense included. Unfortunately, Melina knew better. Their marriage agreement was a practical arrangement, with the added twist of a mutual physical attraction that wasn't going to be satisfied. The problem would be to keep her distance from Adam and still act as if she was wildly in love with him in public.

She gazed thoughtfully as Adam recovered from his coughing fit. She recalled her mother's sage advice that marriage was a matter of compromises. There was a time and a place to get what she wanted, or to even win an argument with her husband, her mother would counsel with a wink. That place to compromise was in the bedroom whern two heads shared the same pillow, her mother always said while a dreamy smile graced her lips.

Too bad she wouldn't have a chance to take advantage of her mother's advice, Melina thought with a quick glance at the interesting cleft in Adam's square chin. A cleft in a man's chin was a sign of strength, her grandmother had told her. Maybe this would be one of those times to compromise, she thought as she gazed at the small piece of honeyed walnut pastry lingering at the corner of his mouth.

One thought led to another until it occurred to her that although Adam had proposed marriage, he had yet to hold her in his arms and kiss her. Her body warmed at the thought of how sweet his lips would have tasted. Of how wonderful it would feel to be held in his arms. Even if it would only be a charade.

This was too public a setting for a kiss to seal their bargain, she realized as she glanced around the roof garden. They were in full view of people on their lunch breaks. The windows of the adjoining Athens Hilton Hotel were only yards away. Close enough for anyone near a window to look out over the vine-covered trellis surrounding the embassy rooftop café. Even the trio of seagulls drawn by the fragrant scent of food seemed to be watching them.

Eleni and Arianna, who were sitting a few feet away, made no attempt to hide their interest in what was going on at her table.

Melina pondered how to play the game without appearing too daring. "My friends are watching," she said uneasily. "Maybe we ought to do something to make things look real?"

"No problem." Adam glanced over at her wide-eyed friends and winked. He took Melina's hand in his and ran his thumb over her velvety skin. Under his breath, and with a wide smile for her friends' benefit, he said, "Melina, are you sure you know what you're doing?"

Melina managed a smile. If a kiss wasn't forth-coming, at least he was holding her hand. She wondered if he knew that tiny electric shocks followed in the path of his large and finely shaped fingers. Or that flashes of erotic thoughts were beginning to turn her limbs to jelly.

"It was your idea to make things look real," she finally choked. "I was only trying to help."

*How far?* her inner voice asked eagerly.

*Not far enough,* her rational mind answered.

"I will take you home to meet my father," she said. She disengaged her tingling hand and hid it in her lap. "I just hope my father doesn't have that heart attack he keeps threatening whenever he doesn't get his way."

"Your father has a heart condition?"

"No, but I'm afraid he will once I bring you home. It's not only you," she hurried to explain. "It's just that you're my choice, not his. Besides, you're not Greek."

Adam still looked doubtful. "Are you sure I have to meet your father? I wouldn't want to be the cause of a heart attack. Maybe we should call the whole thing off."

Maybe, she debated for a brief moment, she should reconsider and let him off the hook. Only there was that green card she yearned for and the chance to be beyond her father's controlling reach.

"As far as I'm concerned, we made an agreement,'' Melina said firmly. ''We have too much at stake to back out now.''

''We have?'' Adam's complexion paled.

Melina gathered her purse and prepared to go back to work. ''Yes, we have. You said you needed a wife. I want a green card. I said I'll marry you, and I will.''

''But your father!''

''Don't worry about my father,'' she said with a frown, ''I'm sure I'll be able to think of something to make it right with him.''

Her father was as healthy as only a man who regularly used virgin olive oil on his food to stay healthy could be. She'd grown up watching her father enjoy his weekly Sunday morning ''medicinal'' breakfast of cucumbers, nuts mixed with yogurt, doused with a liberal portion of Greece's famous virgin olive oil. A man who could survive that kind of regime was surely healthy enough to survive meeting Adam.

Melina rose and waved goodbye to Eleni and Arianna. If she wanted things to look real, she had to wait for Adam to leave with her. ''If you want to make things look real, maybe you ought to walk me back to my desk.''

Adam heard the plea in Melina's voice as he rose from the table. Damn! The woman had taken him seriously when he'd only been kidding. He had a sinking feeling this was his last chance to climb out of the hole he'd dug for himself. But how?

The light in Melina's eyes deterred him from telling her so in public. Especially since Melina was a woman who was frank in her hopes and dreams and who trusted him.

The idea of meeting her father, a traditional Greek man, left a hollow, sinking feeling in his chest. He had to make one last attempt to get her to back out of their agreement.

"Maybe we should elope," he said suddenly. "Tomorrow is Friday. We can get married Saturday night, elope and go on a three-day honeymoon. By the time you tell your father we're married, it'll be too late for him to hassle you."

No sooner had Adam suggested the elopement than he wanted to bite his tongue. Until now he'd prided himself on being honest and pragmatic and definitely a man in control of his life. He was thirty-four, and a successful businessman. And smart enough, he told himself as he glanced down at his "intended," to handle a marriage of convenience, if it came to that, without any complications.

What *was* there about this beautiful, young Greek woman that had caused him to lose his usual self-discipline and to test his sanity? he mused as he followed her into the elevator.

Her smile? The charming way she looked at him under dark eyelashes? The gentle sway of her hips?

What was there in her walk that frankly interested him, when he had no right to be interested?

Her quaint Greek persona? He'd always had an interest in everything Greek, he mused as he tried to reason with himself, or he wouldn't be in the business of importing commodities from Greece.

But a wife he couldn't touch and who looked like Melina? The more he gazed at her, the more he had to smother a desire to take her in his arms and to kiss her senseless.

"Elope? Greek women do not elope!" Melina said, startled at Adam's proposal. She'd been searching for a way to take her mother's advice about compromise, considering Adam's need for a quick marriage. But an elopement?

"Why not? You wanted to get married a moment ago?"

"A marriage, yes. An elopement, no," she agreed, reluctant to let go of the idea of a traditional Greek wedding. Not in church, perhaps, but a wedding with Greek food and hauntingly lovely Greek music. "We have to consider tradition," she sighed, debating the trade-off between settling for a quick wedding ceremony for the chance to realize her dreams. Evidently now was the time to make that compromise. "Okay, I'll agree to the quick wedding, but first, I have to take you home to meet my parents. Would tonight be convenient for you?''

Adam smothered a sigh and reluctantly agreed. There was no use insisting they elope to get Melina to back out of their agreement. She wasn't buying.

On the other hand, what if her father changed Melina's mind for her? What had seemed like a good idea to get her to call off the marriage proposal suddenly turned into an odd sense of loss. To his surprise, he was actually looking forward to having this fascinating woman in his life. One way or another. Even if it meant going by her rules.

"PAPA, MAMMA," Melina said later that night at the door to her family home. "I would like you to meet Adam Blake. Adam is the man I told you about over the telephone. Adam is the man I plan to marry.''

Mikis Kostos eyed him in a way that made Adam uneasy. The uncompromising message in the man's eyes was clear: no man is going to date, let alone marry, my daughter without my approval. From the frown on the man's face, it was also clear to Adam that the chances of his gaining this man's acceptance were slim to none.

"I'm pleased to meet you, sir," Adam said. He didn't go so far as to try to extend his hand, not when Kostos's fists were clenched at his side.

Melina's mother edged closer to her husband. "Mikis?"

It was only after the quiet prompting by Melina's mother that her father held open the door. "Come in, come in," he said. "We don't need to have neighbors watching me be embarrassed by my own daughter."

Adam glanced around at the neighboring houses before he followed Melina into the house. If anyone was watching what was going on on the Kostos's porch, they were either hiding behind bushes or the man was paranoid.

Maybe this visit hadn't been a good idea, after all.

Inside the house, there wasn't a single flat surface not covered with lace doilies and knickknacks of all sizes and shapes. The lamps were topped by upholstered shades with dangling beaded trim. Religious pictures hung on the walls. To Adam, it looked as if time had stood still here while the rest of the world had moved on. No wonder Melina wanted a taste of the twenty-first century before she settled down.

"So, young man, you wish to marry my daughter?"

Adam was taken aback at the speed with which Mikis Kostos cut to the chase. Prompted by Melina's elbow in his ribs, he nodded. "Yes, sir. I do."

"Are you Greek?"

"No, I'm afraid I'm not. I'm an American."

"Your father perhaps is Greek?"

"No, sir. Dad's family came to the United States from England before he was born."

"Your mother is Greek?"

Adam felt as if the walls were beginning to close in on him. It sounded as if Melina's father was about to insist she marry a Greek man loud and long enough for Melina to change her mind about marrying him. "No sir, my mother's family is Irish. In fact, my parents have recently retired to Ireland."

Kostos frowned and looked as if he couldn't find a redeeming branch on Adam's family tree. In the man's mind, Adam was clearly a mongrel. "So tell me, why do you want to marry my Greek daughter?"

Adam glanced at Melina. Now that he'd seen her father, he sympathized with her need for independence. For her sake, he had to find his way through this minefield of a marriage charade without getting married and without hurting Melina.

Melina held up a hand before Adam could answer. "It doesn't matter if Adam isn't Greek, Papa. We've made our decision. Adam has asked me to marry him and I have said yes."

Kostos glowered. "And how does he intend to take care of you?"

It was time for Adam to make a decision, but his pride came first. He reached into his pocket and pulled out his business card. "I have my own import/export business, Mr. Kostos. I import Greek wine, olive oil and other Greek products to the United States. Successfully, I might add."

"Why from Greece? You can get olive oil and wine in Italy, too. Of course—" Kostos huffed his pride "—no one produces virgin olive oil like ours. And my pistachio nuts are the best in the world, too."

"You're right, sir," Adam agreed. Not only because he imported the pistachio nuts, but because he would have agreed to almost anything to end the interview. Before Melina got hurt, he told himself. And, now that he listened to her father, maybe even for his own sake.

"Ah!" Kostos finally nodded approvingly. "It is a good thing you know this. Our women are the most beautiful in the world, too," he said proudly. "No wonder you want to marry my daughter."

With Melina's father's approval of Adam's ability to take care of a wife, Adam realized he was getting too close to becoming a married man again. He glanced over at Melina's mother, Anna. She, to his surprise, was smiling.

"We will talk about a wedding after we have a chance to know you better," Kostos said expansively. "There is plenty of time. My wife and I were neighbors and knew each other for five years before her father consented to our marriage. Now, tell me. When did you and my daughter meet?" he added as he peered at Adam.

Adam was almost speechless. How could he tell Kostos he'd only met the man's daughter today? He looked at Melina for help.

"Peter Stakis introduced us when he visited the embassy," Melina answered, with a fond look at Adam. He knew the look was part of the pretense but it sent his senses spinning anyway. Warning bells rang. "Oh, and by the way, Peter sends you his regards, Papa," she added. "He said to tell you he will visit you soon."

Melina's father appeared to be mollified by the mention of Peter. "Come back for dinner tomorrow, and bring your young man, daughter. We will speak more of this." He glanced at Melina and heaved a deep sigh. "Since Melina is getting older, maybe I will wait only a month or two to give you my answer…"

"I'm sorry, sir," Adam said, afraid it was his last chance to back out of a misguided joke. One failed marriage was enough for him. "We won't be able to come back next Friday. I have to return to the United States next Wednesday."

"To the United States!" The frown reappeared

on Kostos's forehead. "Where in the United States?"

"My home and my business are in San Francisco. It's a large city in northern California," Adam said as he took a step backward at the change that came over the man's face.

"The wedding is off!" Melina's father thundered, waving his hands in the air. Before his fists could fly, her mother rushed to grab her husband by the arm.

"Mikis, no!"

"I do not give you my Greek daughter for you to take away halfway across the world," Kostos said. He glared at Melina. "Of all my children, why is it is you who continues to defy me!"

*Because I am the one most like you,* she wanted to reply. "I'm not defying you, Papa," she retorted. "You said you wanted me to marry and I am. Only to a man of my choice!"

"You go too far," Kostos shouted. "How would I be able to see my grandchildren if you do not live in Greece? Unless," he peered at her, "you are already expecting a baby and do not want me to know."

A baby? Grandchildren! Adam paled.

Melina hurriedly placed herself between her father and him. "You are wrong, Papa. It is only that I gave Adam my word I would marry him, and I will. You are welcome to visit us in the United States.''

The expression on her father's face was clear as he glared at Adam. In the man's opinion, the world had gone to hell, with Adam leading the parade.

There was nothing left to do but make a graceful exit, Adam thought when he felt Melina's warmth against his chest. What really burned him was that Kostos believed he had compromised his daughter.

From the shocked look on Melina's face, Adam sensed there would be no peace for her in her father's house from now on if he walked away from her.

There was no turning back. Charade or not, he owed Melina for putting her in this position. He took her hand in his. ''I'm sorry if you think our cultural differences are that great, Mr. Kostos. And for any wrong ideas you may have about your daughter's honor. In any case, I want to assure you I will take good care of Melina.''

As Adam defended Melina from a position he'd stupidly put her in, he realized he'd forgotten he'd hoped to get out of his proposal. Instead he'd not only defended Melina's honor, it looked as if he'd managed to acquire a wife.

# Chapter Three

On Saturday, Adam breathed a sigh of relief. He'd spent two days obtaining a temporary visa for Melina and a special wedding license. What had started out to be a joke had ended in a real marriage. The brief, impersonal ceremony performed by the American embassy's resident chaplain had thankfully ended almost before it began.

The only thing he seemed to recall clearly was the two floral wreaths Melina had produced for them to wear on their heads. According to his new wife, the wreaths, joined together with white ribbons, were part of the Greek Orthodox wedding ceremony meant to symbolize their new life as a married couple.

Adam hadn't had the heart to remind Melina that this was a marriage in name only—a marriage that could be dissolved as soon as she obtained her green card. Considering the hurried ceremony, he supposed that wearing the wreath was the least he could have done for her.

"Thank you for helping out on such short notice," Adam said gratefully to his best man, Peter Stakis. Eleni Leontis and Arianna Miscouri, the happy bridesmaids, let out squeals of happiness and rushed forward to hug the blushing bride.

"My pleasure, my friend," Peter answered, obviously puzzled at the unexpected result of Adam's meeting with Melina only three days ago, but too much of a gentleman to comment. "But you've forgotten something. You have yet to kiss the bride!"

Adam, who had been wondering just how long he would be able to keep his hands off his new wife, glanced at Melina. A kiss to seal their bargain? Why not? According to their agreement, kissing in public was legit. Besides, the undercurrent of sensual attraction between himself and Melina was definitely real even if their marriage was not.

"You're right. Pardon me, ladies." Adam pulled his unresisting new bride to his side, put his arms around her shoulders and kissed her. Gently, not only for the benefit of their audience, but because he wasn't sure about Melina's reaction. When she gazed up at him with those intriguing lavender eyes, he did what he'd wanted to do for the past three days. He deepened the kiss until Melina's lips stirred under his.

Their marriage might only be one of convenience, he mused as he gazed down at the surprised look on Melina's face, but it seemed to him she had enjoyed the kiss as much as he had.

If only he hadn't been foolish enough to agree to be a hands-off groom to a bride whose lips begged to be kissed. To complicate matters, the way she was gazing back at him was doing a number on his testosterone level.

For a moment he actually felt guilty about taking advantage of Melina, but he didn't regret the kiss. When she pulled away, he filed the kiss under "unfinished business."

As he listened to the minister's small talk, Adam kept an appreciative eye on his bride. She wore a short, white, silk slip of a dress. A matching sheer scarf embroidered with tiny pink roses covered her bare, creamy shoulders. A floral wreath of pink roses woven in between tiny green ferns encircled her shining dark brown hair.

It wasn't her mother's wedding gown, which she'd hoped to wear on her wedding day, he'd overheard Melina lament to her friends before the ceremony. The off-the-rack dress had been all she could find to resemble a wedding dress on short notice, she'd said.

His usual dark blue business suit, white shirt and blue-and-white striped tie suited him just fine. But, what *was* embarrassing had been the duplicate floral wreaths Melina had produced for them to wear on their heads during the ceremony. He'd been tempted to beg off, but considering how much of a traditional Greek wedding Melina had given up by agreeing to today's ceremony, he'd caved in.

Girls seemed to be made of more than sugar and spice, he thought as he gazed at his bride out of the corner of his eye. They were the weavers of dreams and the stuff that could hold a marriage together— if their husbands were willing to cooperate. With one failed marriage behind him, he was afraid this marriage, real or not, wasn't destined to fare any better than his first.

He couldn't remember ever having seen a more beautiful bride than Melina, he thought as she laughed at something Arianna said, blushed then glanced at him. He tried to look as if he hadn't noticed, but it didn't take much imagination to guess that the remark had been about the wedding night.

If this had been a real marriage, he would have been looking forward to the wedding night and the short honeymoon. Instead, since he *was* an honorable man, it was going to have to be hands off his bride, with an annulment somewhere down the line. He didn't need the complications of having to go through another divorce. One had been bad enough.

One step at a time, he told himself. One step at a

time. What he had to do was to somehow get through the rest of the evening and the brief honeymoon without touching his new wife. It wasn't going to be easy, he thought ruefully when his body stirred at the sound of Melina's fresh burst of laughter.

Maybe it was just as well the marriage *was* temporary, he mused wryly. He wasn't husband material. A woman deserved something more than a husband who spent two out of four weeks on the go. At least, that's what his ex had said when she'd asked for a divorce.

In spite of his attempt at pragmatic rationalization, the idea of a temporary, unconsummated marriage didn't sound as sensible now as it had before. Not when the bride had already made giant inroads to his psyche.

He told himself Melina would get something out of the marriage—a green card. In fact, he'd already started the paperwork to get one for her as the wife of an American citizen. The way bureaucratic red tape usually inched along, he was afraid that the two-year mandatory wait was going to be trouble.

"Congratulations, my friend," Peter said after he'd rejoined Adam. "Who would have thought an unromantic and pragmatic American like yourself would fall in love with a romantic Greek woman, and at first sight?" He stood back and regarded

Adam with a quizzical look. "And even to agree to wear the traditional wedding wreath."

Adam shrugged and glanced at the beribboned wreaths Melina now held in her hand. "It was Melina's idea. I understand the custom brings good luck to a marriage," he said, knowing he'd been a fraud to have agreed to wear the wreath.

Peter was right about him, Adam thought as he studied his beautiful bride. He always prided himself on being honest and straightforward to a fault. His friends had accused him of being overly cautious, straitlaced and without a sense of humor.

If they could only see him now.

"Wait a moment," Melina called, rushing to his side. She took a rose out of one of the wreaths and tucked it into the buttonhole in his lapel. "There," she said with a shy smile. "Something for you to remember this day."

Adam looked into Melina's intriguing lavender eyes—and all his nerve ends began to tingle. Real marriage or not, he wouldn't need the rose to help him remember today's wedding. Or that she was his wife. She was the kind of woman a red-blooded man would never forget.

Melina saw a fleeting look of regret flit over Adam's eyes. If he was having second thoughts about their marriage bargain, she hoped it wasn't because of her. She intended to be a good wife to

Adam even if their bargain called for sleeping on separate pillows.

"Is something wrong?"

"Not really." Adam made a show of glancing at his watch. "I was just thinking it's about time to set off on our honeymoon."

Melina's mind whirled at the word "honeymoon" and all its usual connotations. The way Adam had kissed her and the way he was looking at her now made her hormones stand at attention. He had to be the temptation her strict father had warned her against, but at the moment she didn't care. Too bad she'd asked for a no-touching rule, she thought as she thrust temptation behind her for now. "Where are we going?"

"I have a friend, Yannis Alexacki. He's offered to lend us his villa on Corfu."

Melina felt herself blanch and her stomach roil at the mention of Corfu. Any sensuous thoughts she might have entertained at the thought of really honeymooning with Adam flew out of her mind. "Corfu?"

"Yes. Yannis has become a good friend over the years. He'll be able to swear we're in love and on a real honeymoon."

"A witness? To our honeymoon?"

Adam fought back the smile at the look on Melina's face. "Don't worry. Once he gives us the key, he'll leave us alone." *And so will I,* he added to remind himself this was to be a platonic marriage. When Melina didn't look convinced, he tried to reassure her. "I arranged a honeymoon for a reason. When the United States Immigration department investigates us for your green card, Peter can swear he witnessed our wedding and Yannis will be able to swear we honeymooned at his villa."

"But, Corfu is an island!" she blurted.

Adam looked confused. "Right. Any problem with that?"

Melina was too embarrassed to tell Adam she became seasick just thinking of a boat. "We go by boat?"

"Don't worry," Adam assured her. "The voyage to Corfu doesn't take too long."

"Long enough," Melina muttered.

"You're not having second thoughts, are you? I'm afraid it's a little too late to cancel now."

"No. It's just that I tend to get a little seasick," Melina said bravely. What man wanted a seasick bride on a honeymoon, even if the honeymoon wasn't going to be a real one? She'd come this far to escape her father and an arranged marriage—now was not the time to think of turning back. "I'm ready to leave whenever you are."

Adam motioned to the wedding guests. "We'll leave just as soon as we say goodbye."

"You can't leave now," Eleni protested when she heard Adam's plans for a honeymoon. "It's a custom in our country for the bride and groom to share a meal together at their wedding."

Melina glanced at Adam. "Do we have time?"

By now Adam had had all the Greek customs and promises he could handle, including Melina's no-touching rule. He tried to look like an eager bridegroom. "Thank you, but we have a boat to catch."

With a dramatic sigh, Eleni dug into her purse and pulled out little paper bags filled with rice and tied with ribbons. After passing them to Peter and Arianna, she blew air kisses at Adam and Melina and, shouting, *"Hopa!"* she tossed the rice into the air. "May you be blessed with many children!"

Melina's smile faded as she glanced at Adam and saw a startled look come over his face. He was right. With the no-touching rule, there would be no chance of their having children. The idea of a son that resembled Adam made her ache with a longing she'd never taken the time to dwell on before. Even though the rule had been her idea, after promising to love, honor and cherish Adam, she was almost ready to change her mind if he asked her to.

Adam swallowed hard as a grain of rice hit him above his right eye. He wasn't going to stick around to hear any Greek blessings, tradition or not. Children! Fat chance, when he thought of his promise not to touch his bride. Besides, his daughter Jamie was enough for him. He reached for Melina's hand and dashed with her out of the chapel.

As if her fear of water had become a prophecy, Melina leaned limply over the side of the ferryboat taking them to Corfu. "I'm sorry," she whispered. "I took the seasick pills you gave me before we left, but they don't seem to be working."

"Don't worry about it." Working on the theory that they were still in public and that touching was okay, Adam joined her on the bench and offered his handkerchief. "If I'd known you'd react this way, I would have arranged to fly to the island."

Melina dabbed at her lips and smiled wearily. "I'm sure I'll be fine as soon as we get on land."

"Good." Adam felt relieved, but he wasn't so sure she was right. She was a good sport and deserved better than to be taken on a ferryboat that not only transported humans but also accommodated livestock.

He eyed a family huddled together across the deck. An older boy had a small pig trapped in his arms. A young sibling held the tether to a goat while his mother, from her gestures, warned him to be sure the goat didn't chew its way free.

To really blow Adam's mind, the goat was watching him intently.

"Yannis has arranged to have the ferryboat stop at his private dock," Adam said with a watchful eye on the goat. "He said he would only hang around long enough to take us to his villa. I'm sure you'll feel much better after a good night's sleep." He put his hand under her hair and gently massaged the back of her neck.

He heard a gentle sigh as Melina settled against him. The rapid rise and fall of her breasts against his chest gradually slowed to an even, steady beat. Surprised by her sudden silence, he gazed down at his new bride. The seasick pills must have finally worked; she'd actually fallen asleep in his arms. He raised his other hand to gently caress her cheek. Touching was okay, he told himself. They were, after all, in public.

Suddenly he felt something nudge his back. When he turned around, there was the bewhiskered goat actually trying to reach the rose Adam wore in his lapel!

He let out a curse. The boy's mother grabbed her son by his ear and, with an apologetic smile, pointed to Adam's jacket.

Adam tore the rose from his coat lapel, tossed it at the goat and shielded Melina before the animal had a chance to go for the small wedding bouquet she clutched in her hand.

Adam mentally compared the voyage to the uneventful ferry back home that ran between San Francisco and Sausalito. Cars and people, yes. Livestock, no. So much for quaint Greek customs.

Thankfully, Yannis, as good as his word, was waiting at his private dock where he had arranged for a special ferry stop.

Melina looked so peaceful nestled against him, Adam hated to wake her. He gathered her in his arms, motioned to an attendant to bring their two small bags and strode off the boat to meet his friend. "Thanks, Yannis. I'm sorry my wife isn't awake to meet you," he said, determined to have his friend believe Melina was a much-loved bride.

"Ah," Yannis said with a broad smile. "The honeymoon has begun?"

Adam glanced down at long brown eyelashes that curved against Melina's flushed cheeks. "I wish," he said dryly. "I'm afraid my wife was seasick coming over. What she needs now is a good night's rest on firm ground."

Yannis took the two bags from the ferry attendant and motioned for Adam to follow. "I've arranged for your privacy. I have given the servants the weekend off," he said expansively. "There's enough food and drink to last you for a few days, my friend. Although I don't suppose you will be interested in food at a time like this. The rest of the honeymoon is up to you." He winked.

*I wish,* Adam thought as he shifted a sleeping Melina more comfortably in his arms. He followed his friend up the lighted stairs that had been carved into the hillside.

On the first level he reached, there was a large swimming pool surrounded by a cabana and white-and-green patio furniture. The approach to the villa itself—on the next level—was lined by graceful Greek statues and towering white marble columns covered with flowering honeysuckle vines. A beautiful blue sea and a white beach came into view.

As he realized they had reached the open interior of the villa overlooking the Ionian Sea he wished Melina was awake to enjoy the view. A few more steps and he found himself in a bedroom with a large king-size bed covered with a blue-and-white-velvet bedspread and matching pillows. The outer wall was a large picture window open to the scented evening air.

Adam's body hardened at the impossible thought of lying against the mound of soft pillows and gazing out over the horizon with Melina in his arms.

Yannis stood aside while Adam gently placed Melina on the bed. "Nice, yes?"

"Nice, yes," Adam echoed with a wry glance at his sleeping bride. "Is there another bedroom?"

"Another bedroom?" Yannis grinned. "There is only one bedroom here," he added with a wink.

"What would a bachelor like myself need with two bedrooms?"

Adam's heart sank. The bed, certainly more than large enough to accommodate two people, was a temptation. But what if Melina awakened to find him in bed with her? More to the point, if he slept with her, how would he be able to keep to the no-touching rule?

Yet there was no way he was looking forward to sleeping on a couch in the other room tonight. After the surprising events of the past three days, he was simply exhausted.

"Well, my friend," Yannis said cheerfully, "I will leave you to your honeymoon. There is a private telephone line in the den linked to my office in town, call me when you're ready to leave."

Adam was almost sorry to see his friend go. The immediate problem now was that he and Melina would be alone. And once they had their privacy, the damned no-touching rule would kick in.

A promise was a promise, he told himself as he turned back to the bedroom. It didn't mean he had to like it.

In the meantime it was up to him to make sure Melina was comfortable. With the household help gone, the job was now his.

The no-touching rule would have to be suspended for now.

He mentally crossed his fingers for luck, took a deep breath and slipped off Melina's shoes. It took a few moments for him to determine what came next, but he decided the obvious place to start was with her legs. He gently peeled silk stockings down long, shapely, creamy-smooth legs and over slender ankles to manicured toes.

The zipper on her sheer white dress presented a problem. He studied the dress before he gently turned Melina onto her side and slowly pulled down the zipper to below her waist. To his relief, Melina sighed and turned over onto her back. Sliding the dress off her shoulders and down her slender hips was a breeze.

He studied her sheer lacy bra and panties. They would prove to be a major problem that he was currently in no condition to try to resolve if he intended to honor their bargain. He left the dainty garments on, gently pulled the bedcovers back and arranged his sleeping bride in a cocoon of soft throw pillows.

Melina was everything a sane man could want in a woman, he thought as he gazed down at her. He questioned his sanity for putting himself in such a no-win situation as this. There was absolutely no way he could join her in bed and honor their bargain.

To keep himself awake, he wandered into a gleaming kitchen to find something to eat. Copper pots and pans hung from racks above the stove. A coffeemaker, a sealed canister of coffee and a toaster waited on a tiled counter.

A note on the refrigerator caught his attention. To his surprise, and great relief, it was an invitation to help himself.

Too tired to investigate the entire contents of the refrigerator, Adam reached inside for a covered plate of sliced chicken breast and an apple to munch on while he considered where to sleep.

He wandered from room to room. Unless he was a contortionist, the sectional couch in the living room was out. The couch in the den, which was no more than a futon covered with colorful pillows, resembled more of a playground than a bed.

A large TV stood against one den wall. A movie screen and a wall of built-in shelves containing dozens of videos filled another. Like the bedroom, an entire wall was made of glass.

Yannis had been dead-on about the secluded villa being a bachelor pad, Adam thought wearily as he made his way back to the kitchen—the only enclosed room in the house.

If he wanted a good night's sleep, he had to go back to the bedroom and find a way to share the only decent bed in the house.

Adam stood at the foot of the bed, contemplating Melina. He finally decided he could resort to the early American custom of "bundling" he'd read about in some history class years ago. With beds scarce in Colonial America, he remembered reading that guests slept in the same beds separated by a barrier.

With the abundance of available pillows, Adam carefully created a barrier down the middle of the bed. Safe enough, he thought as he took off his outer garments, undershirt, shoes and socks. Clad only in his boxers he climbed into his half of the bed and covered himself with a throw he had found on a chair.

He tried to relax. But there was a problem. Melina's scent was driving him wild. Even though his rational mind said no to erotic thoughts, his body kept saying yes.

How was he going to last until the "honeymoon" was over two days from now? he wondered. He finally turned his back to Melina, but it didn't seem to help. He hadn't been able to keep his eyes open a minute ago and now he couldn't close them.

*"Adam, agape mou,"* Melina whispered in her sleep. "Hold me, my love."

Adam froze when Melina spoke Greek in her sleep. He knew enough of the language to know *agape mou* meant "my love," but the invitation to hold her? The idea was tempting, but he couldn't take advantage of a sleeping woman. Could he?

He had to stop thinking of Melina as his bride.

He waited until he was sure Melina was asleep before he felt safe enough to close his eyes. But not until he reminded himself to be up and out of bed before Melina awakened. How could he possibly explain a quaint American custom like bundling to his Greek bride?

The last thing he thought of before he fell asleep was that awake or asleep Melina was sexy as hell.

DAWN WAS BREAKING when Melina awakened. Disoriented by the strange surroundings, she lay there, testing her queasy stomach. "Thank you," she murmured when it remained quiet. She tried to remember where she was and came up blank.

What she did realize, after a cautious glance, was that she was somewhere in bed with Adam Blake, her convenient husband. Not only in bed, but that they were hip to hip, leg to leg and ankle to ankle under a jumble of blankets and small pillows. To make things even more surprising, her cheek rested on Adam's masculine chest while his arm spanned her waist!

She had to be dreaming, she told herself as she slid a hand across his chest. There was no way that, awake, she would have had the courage to explore the curves at his lithe waist, to run her fingers through the golden-brown curls on his very masculine chest, or to inhale his masculine scent of shaving lotion and soap. Or to touch the nipples that sprang to life at her touch.

The nipples hardened!

Melina shot out of bed, grabbed the first item of clothing large enough to cover her, and pulled on Adam's shirt.

She tried to remember what had happened last night. After mentally taking an inventory of the way she felt, she relaxed. The night had passed in a blur, but she was still innocent.

For that matter, most of the past three days since she'd met Adam in the embassy elevator seemed to have passed in a blur.

Fool that she was, she hadn't taken the time to consider that her plan to go to the United States to work as Adam's housekeeper/nanny could backfire and turn her into the true wife of a man she hardly knew. She covered her lips with trembling fingers.

"Adam! You have to wake up!"

Adam opened his eyes. The first thing he saw were long, slender legs and a shirt that barely covered shapely thighs. Blinking, his gaze moved upward to take in the rest of Melina. She was standing over him with fire in her eyes.

"It's not what you think," he began as he struggled to sit up in bed. "I can explain."

"Explain!" She motioned to the rumpled bed. "How can you explain that?"

"I swear there was nowhere else to sleep, at least comfortably," he said as he tried to concentrate. "I was worn out, so I decided to sleep here with you. But not before I made a barrier between us. In the early days of my country, it was called bundling."

"Bundling? A barrier?" Her eyes narrowed as she searched the bed. "I see no barrier."

"The pillows were the barrier." He glanced around him and saw a tumbled mound of pillows that in no way made two beds out of the one. "I swear I put pillows between us," he said, raking his hands through his hair. "It was the only way I could think of not to touch you."

He looked so chagrined, Melina was tempted to forgive him. Just as she had to forgive herself for putting herself in this position. She grabbed her small suitcase and looked around for an adjoining bathroom. "I'm going to shower and change. You may do as you wish."

Adam peered at her as she struggled to cover her bare hips with his shirt. One thing was for sure, he had to get home to the United States as fast as possible.

At the rate he was going, getting back to a less romantic setting was the only way to keep his sanity.

## Chapter Four

Thirty-six hours later, Melina was standing in the spacious living room of Adam's San Francisco town house. The flights from Athens to San Francisco had largely passed in a polite, awkward silence. Maybe because underneath Adam's polite small talk, he felt bewildered by their one-day honeymoon back in Corfu. She certainly knew she was.

Even now, Melina tried to convince herself that finding herself in bed with Adam's arms around her had only been a dream. She knew better. Even if it had only been a dream, it had to have been something she'd subconsciously wanted or she wouldn't have given in to the desire to cuddle close to him. Or to run her fingers through the golden-brown curls on his chest in her dream.

"Well, this is the place I call home," Adam said, closing the door behind her. He glanced around the quiet rooms, lit only by the fading rays of sunshine.

"I hope you'll be comfortable here. Just let me know if there's anything you want or need."

Melina glanced around the room. How unlived-in the place looked. What she'd hoped to find was a real home, not one that resembled a sterile hotel suite. She sighed.

In Adam, she'd hoped to find a man who, if he didn't want a real wife, would in time at least become a friend. One who would help her find her place in a new world. Instead, awake or asleep, Adam had turned out to be a package of sensuality no woman in her right mind could resist. Including, to her chagrin, her.

She'd hoped to get to know Adam during their honeymoon, to understand him, but the honeymoon hadn't lasted long enough. It hadn't worked. Even after being carried away by his proximity and breaking her own no-touching-in-private rule, she realized they remained further apart than ever.

They'd been strangers when they met and were strangers still. It's better this way, she told herself firmly. It will be easier to leave him when the time comes.

Adam dropped their suitcases in an adjoining room and came back to stride into the compact open kitchen. "I'm afraid you won't find much in the way of foodstuff. I'm not home enough to bother fixing much for myself." He glanced at the row of near-empty, glass-fronted cupboards. "With you and Jamie here for the summer," he said with a wry smile, "I guess I should do something about that right away."

Melina took stock of her surroundings. He was right. The town house and its pristine small kitchen reflected the lifestyle of a single man who was seldom home. It looked as if he did need a housekeeper and a nanny. But did he need a wife?

She opened a pantry door to find the space largely bare. She thought of the many times her mother had made peace with her father by cooking him one of his favorite meals. Maybe she could do the same with Adam. On the other hand, it looked as if the chances of successfully trying her mother's cure on Adam might be a waste of time. Adam clearly wasn't ready to tell.

"We can go shopping now, if you have time," she said, trying to ignore the tug that pulled at her heart just thinking of how empty Adam's life must have been without his family around him. "I will make dinner while you pick up Jamie. What does she like to eat?"

Adam raked his fingers through his hair. "Frankly, I wasn't around enough to pay much attention. Macaroni and cheese? I know she likes a snack of cookies and milk before bedtime."

She glanced at Adam. "Is there a grocery store

close by where we can shop? I will need the ingredients to make *kourabiethes,* Greek butter cookies.''

"Cookies?'' Adam looked startled at her suggestion. "Are you sure you're not too tired to start baking? Can't it wait?''

"No. I want to teach your little girl to bake the cookies. Baking together is a way of bonding. I learned to bake at my mother's side when I was Jamie's age.''

"Okay, but I don't have a clue what you need to make Greek cookies,'' he answered before he brightened. "I just remembered. There's a small Greek store a couple of blocks away. They ought to have everything you need.''

"The grocery will be fine.'' She listed the ingredients she needed. "And a small amount of brandy.''

"Brandy?'' He glanced at a picture of Jamie on a nearby shelf. "The kid is only six. Are you sure about the brandy?''

"Very sure,'' Melina followed his gaze. "Don't worry. I only use a small amount. It is what keeps the cookies moist and makes them taste so good.''

"Got it.'' Adam wasn't so sure about the brandy, but after glimpsing a side of Melina on their shortened honeymoon that he hadn't suspected existed, it had already begun to dawn on him that his impulsive offer of a marriage of convenience wasn't going to be boring. Baking cookies with Jamie. There was more to his bride than he'd suspected.

"There's brandy around here somewhere. We can get the rest of the stuff at the mom-and-pop grocery."

"What is this mom-and-pop store?" A frown crossed Melina's forehead. "A place where a mother sells drinks? I'm afraid we will need more than sodas."

Adam smiled at the expression on Melina's face. She'd never looked more appealing. "Sorry, I keep forgetting you're not used to our local expressions. A mom-and-pop store is where the proprietors run a small business."

Melina dimpled. "I am afraid I have a lot to learn about American language. You will have to put up with me while I do."

Put up with her? Adam smothered a groan, remembering her velvet-soft skin when he'd leaned over her in that sensuous setting in Corfu.

If she only knew! He not only liked her, he was becoming more and more attracted to her. How to avoid showing how he felt was the problem. For a man who prided himself on his common sense, here he was behaving like an untried schoolboy.

"Ready to go?"

"Ready." She smiled and slung the straps of her purse over her shoulder.

She looked so appealing with the eager smile that lit up her face that Adam almost forgot what he'd just told himself. What he really wanted was to gather her in his arms and to kiss those adorable dimples that danced on her cheeks.

He motioned her out the door and took great care not to touch her.

As they entered the small Papadakis Market, he heard Melina's sigh of pleasure. He couldn't blame her, he thought as he inhaled the spicy scents that filled the air. It had been his discovery of the little store that had firmed his determination to become an importer of Greek products. Four years later, he'd never turned back.

The store's wooden planks had absorbed years of fragrant spices. Shelves held cans labeled Elliniko Café, which he knew meant Greek coffee. There were other shelves filled with small canvas bags of nuts—particularly pistachios—and next to them, large tin cans of Greek virgin olive oil. Barrels held salted fish and pickles. Jars held grape leaves tenderized in brine. Shelves of dried spices in plastic bags sat alongside packages of Greek sea salt and seasonings.

To whet a shopper's appetite, there were trays of baklava, his favorite, and several kinds of hard cookies. Bottle after bottle of Retsina, Ouzo and fine

Greek wines filled shelves. Ready-made appetizers-to-go waited under glass-covered trays.

Melina stopped in front of enameled containers of Greek feta cheese, took a deep breath and smiled her delight.

Adam was happy to see the pleasure in her eyes. At the same time, he felt uneasy for taking her out of her native environment and into a culture where she might feel like a fish out of water. "Go ahead. Buy anything that suits your fancy. Just don't forget the stuff to make those cookies for Jamie."

The store's proprietor, Josef Papadakis himself, sailed out from behind a counter. "Ah, my friend the importer! What do you have to offer me today?"

"Not a thing." Adam smiled as he shook the man's hand, "Just shopping. I would like to introduce you to my wife," he said, reaching for Melina. "Melina, I'd like you to meet Joe Papadakis, the owner of this paradise. Joe, my wife. Melina is from Athens."

Papadakis smiled broadly. He took Melina's hand and kissed her fingertips. "That is good! A Greek wife is a treasure, no?" he asked in Greek.

"Yes," Adam replied in English, grinning at the blush that came over Melina's face at the praise. He stored away the information that it didn't take much to make her happy. Just a nice phrase now and again. "We just arrived this afternoon. Melina needed a few things to make dinner. Oh, and cookies. Just charge them to me.''

"More than a few, I am afraid," Melina said with a helpless shrug. "The house is empty."

"No problem!" Papadakis waved expansively to their surroundings. "My store is yours!"

"Thank you. Just a few things to start with for now, please."

Papadakis nodded. "First, we celebrate your marriage." He hurried to the tray of appetizers and brought back a small slice of baklava on a paper plate. "May your marriage be as sweet," he said, handing the plate to Melina.

She smiled, made a token bite into the pastry and passed the plate to Adam. *"Nai, poli nostimo,"* she murmured. "Yes, very delicious," she added in English as a courtesy to Adam.

Adam smothered a grin. He wasn't exactly fluent in the Greek language, but he was able to understand enough to get by. He liked the way she took pains to translate for him. No way was he going to give himself away.

Papadakis beamed and gestured around the shop. "Come, shop, shop. Your new husband can wait."

An hour later, laden with fragrant groceries and munching on the storekeeper's largess, they were back in the town house.

"I'd better go get Jamie," Adam said with a glance at his watch. "Will you be okay?"

Her nose in one of the shopping bags, Melina nodded happily.

With a lingering look behind him, Adam left to bring home the reason for his convenient marriage. The problem was, he mused as he drove his car out of the downstairs garage, the marriage of convenience might be convenient, but it didn't look as if it was going to be all that satisfying.

HUMMING UNDER HER BREATH, Melina put the perishables in the refrigerator, the canned goods and canvas bags of nuts and spices in the pantry. She actually liked Adam, she thought as she assembled the ingredients to make his favorite moussaka. More than liked him, she thought with a blush. After the Corfu fiasco, however, he'd made it clear he'd married her to get a nanny for his daughter, not a wife.

Even a marriage of convenience came with its own set of problems, she mused unhappily. Especially when she didn't have a clue as to how her "husband" actually felt about her. The overt sensual glances when he thought she wasn't looking were definitely part of the problem. Her instinctive reaction to those glances was to say yes, even while her rational mind said no. Marriage without the heart and soul engaged was no marriage at all.

Adam couldn't possibly want her as a real wife, she told herself once the moussaka was inside the oven. She strolled into the living room. After all, he was a twenty-first-century man, and she was still mired in the old-fashioned traditions of a small Greek village.

Even so, given the right signals, she thought as she picked up the tie Adam had carelessly thrown on a chair, she would have been happy to be a true wife.

She gazed out the large picture window that over-looked the striking orange bridge their pilot had identified as the Golden Gate Bridge as they'd circled the city before landing. The street below the window teemed with cars, its sidewalks with pedestrians. The hills on the horizon were covered with side-by-side apartment houses with room to spare. Just like Athens, but foggy and cold. A ferryboat with colorful flags streaming from its pilot house crossed the bay.

Wistfully, she compared the busy waterfront with the dazzling clear blue Ionian Sea that surrounded Corfu. And the beautiful sandy beach below the villa she, because of her actions, hadn't been able to enjoy.

Instead of commercial development, the northern side of the island, facing Italy, had been covered with lush vineyards and fruit and olive trees.

And yet, the scene in front of her still reminded her of Athens, a city trying to transform itself for the new century and the coming Olympics. A wave of homesickness came over her.

What had she gotten herself into? Melina wondered as she wandered into the bedroom where Adam had left her luggage. To her dismay, it contained a single king-size bed, just as in Corfu. Another invitation for trouble.

A wry smile curved her lips as she wondered if Adam had realized they would have to share that bed. Unless he slept on the couch in the living room. With the need to maintain the facade of a happy marriage, it looked as if they'd have no other choice.

Maybe, she thought as she tried to avoid looking at the bed, it would help to get to know each other. And yet, she mused unhappily, Adam had already made it clear there was no future for their marriage.

Melina was hanging her dresses in the clothes closet when Adam returned with his daughter, a small female replica of himself, complete with his hazel eyes, golden-brown hair and dimple in her tiny chin.

''Melina, I'd like to introduce you to my daughter, Jamie.''

Melina smiled her welcome and held out her hand. ''I'm very pleased to meet you, Jamie.'' To her surprise, the little girl backed away and hid behind her father.

Adam frowned. "Jamie?" When she didn't reply, he pulled her around to stand in front of him. "Melina's come all the way from Greece to take care of you. What's wrong?"

The little girl hung back. Clutching a small doll to her chest, her wide eyes gave her thoughts away. She had already decided not to like Melina. "I don't need anyone to take care of me. I already have a mother!"

Startled at the fierce determination in the child's voice, Melina felt herself blanch. "I never meant to say I was—"

Adam broke in before she could finish her sentence. "Jamie! What made you say something like that?"

"Because Mommy told me you got married again and that you're probably going to start a new family." Tears clung to the corners of Jamie's hazel eyes as she gazed up at her father. "Does that mean you don't want me for your little girl anymore?"

Adam smothered an oath, swung Jamie into his arms and covered her face with kisses. "Want you for my little girl? Of course I want you, sweetheart. You'll be my girl forever. You've misunderstood Mommy. Sure, I got married again, but I want you so much, I've even made arrangements with your mommy to have you stay with me through the whole summer.''

Melina's heart ached for little Jamie. She reminded her of herself at the same age when, for almost five years, she'd been a pampered only child. Of her bewilderment at the changes in the attention she received from her parents once her brother, Andreas, was born. And again when two years later her younger brother, Christos, followed.

Her heart ached as she realized how she'd been fooling herself into believing she hadn't been ready to become a mother and to start a family of her own. A family she would never have as long as she remained married to Adam.

''Perhaps we can be friends?'' Melina forced a smile and held out a hand to Jamie. ''I will tell you all about my country while you tell me all about yours. I will also show you how to make Greek cookies. No?''

At the mention of cookies, Jamie cautiously peeked at Melina. ''No mommy? Just friends?''

''No mommy,'' Melina echoed as she met Jamie's wary eyes. ''Just friends. If you like, we can begin by baking cookies together later.''

Jamie nodded, obviously interested by the mention of cookies. But Melina still saw the wary look in her eyes.

Now that the two women in his life had met and

established a tenuous relationship, Adam felt like a bigger fraud than ever. He wasn't prepared to admit to himself, let alone to Melina, that he hoped Jamie's presence would help him keep his distance from his inconvenient bride. After his unexpected physical reaction to Melina, he figured he needed all the help he could muster to keep their marriage platonic.

It had been years since he'd been so attracted to a woman, including his ex, he mused as he watched Melina lead Jamie to the kitchen. And not only because his Greek "wife" was beautiful. She was much more than that. Smart, interesting and, in her quaint, foreign way, funny. He was so attracted to her that, instead of trying to keep his promise not to touch her in private, he wanted to take her in his arms to show her what a real marriage could be.

The thought brought up another problem, one he hadn't taken the time to dwell on before. And certainly not before he'd realized how much he was beginning to enjoy having Melina in his life. It was a problem he hoped hadn't yet occurred to Melina or there would be hell to pay. An annulment somewhere down the line would play havoc with her chances of getting a green card, let alone destroy her trust in him. Even a divorce, if they consummated their "marriage," would muddy the waters.

From the shy looks Jamie was sending Melina, he

sensed the beginnings of a tenuous friendship was about to grow between them. A friendship that might eventually tempt him into a relationship he'd had no plans to pursue.

As for seducing Melina… Not in this lifetime, he told himself. But what could he do to ensure Melina would eventually be granted a green card as he'd promised?

She couldn't claim political asylum—not with Greece on the list of friendly countries.

Waiting for a lottery was another dubious choice. One way or another, they had to prove Melina was the happily married spouse of a U.S. citizen for her to move to the top of the waiting list.

MELINA BUSIED HERSELF showing Jamie how to make *kourabiethes*. Jamie's small fingers flew as, with Melina guiding her, she mixed the butter and sugar, stirred in an egg yolk and carefully kneaded the dough before she shaped the small crescent cookies.

"You are a fine cook, Jamie. You learn fast," Melina announced. "I hope I learn your American expressions as quickly."

Jamie bounced happily at the praise, but all Adam could think of were the fine lines of Melina's slender neck as she bent over Jamie's shoulder. And the way her hair fell across her sparkling lavender eyes.

"And now, dinner," Melina announced when the

cookies were ready to go into the oven before they were dusted with powdered sugar, even though Jamie had eaten enough raw cookie dough to be full. "Maybe a sandwich?"

By the time Jamie had eaten half a grilled-cheese sandwich and the Greek cookies had been dusted with powdered sugar and sampled, she was yawning into her glass of milk.

Melina smiled as she gently brushed a smudge of powdered sugar off the little girl's forehead. "Poor little darling. I'm afraid there is more powdered sugar on her than on the cookies." She took the half full glass of milk from Jamie's limp hand, washed the powdered sugar off her face and traded gentle glances with Adam. "I'll get her bed ready. You can carry her to her room."

"Sure." Impressed with Melina's interaction with Jamie, Adam picked up his daughter and headed for the smaller of the two bedrooms. It looked as if he'd lucked out in his choice of a wife, after all. Melina was not only a loving woman, he could see she took her new position in Jamie's life seriously. More seriously than he had when he'd blithely followed his friend Peter's lead and proposed marriage to a woman he'd only known for a few hours.

Sexual attraction aside, he suddenly felt the need to get to know Melina better. Not only for his daughter's sake, he realized as he carried the little girl into the bedroom, but for his own.

"There's no point in disturbing her tonight, she's been through a lot today," Melina murmured as she gently took off Jamie's shoes and socks. "We can give her a bath in the morning.

"It can't be easy for her to meet the woman she thinks might replace her mother in her life," she went on.

"It's always been one step forward and two steps backward with Jamie," Adam said ruefully as he gazed down at his sleeping daughter. "At least, since her mother and I were divorced two years ago."

Melina tucked the covers around Jamie and led the way out of the bedroom. "Perhaps things will change now."

Adam sighed and glanced over his shoulder. "The divorce wasn't my idea. I was too busy setting up my business to realize how it was affecting my marriage. I should have known better."

Melina sank onto the couch, prepared to listen and to learn more about the real Adam under that businesslike facade. "Not intentionally, I'm sure."

"Maybe, maybe not," Adam said as he strode back and forth across the room and stopped to gaze out the window. "Jeanette claimed I was away too much and for too long at a time. She wanted a husband who was available twenty-four seven.''

"Twenty-four seven? Another one of your strange expressions!'' Melina shook her head. ''What does it mean?''

Adam grinned and turned away from the picture window. There was nothing better to lighten his mood than Melina's quaint reactions to the everyday expressions he used so freely. ''It means twenty four hours a day, seven days a week, without a stop. Maybe a nine-to-five job would have made the grade with Jeanette,'' he went on. ''To please her, I went to work as a sales manager in a import and export company for a time. After I discovered how much I wanted to start my own company, I quit and went into business for myself.'' He shrugged. ''I couldn't accommodate my ex and still keep up with my business working part-time.''

"Jamie is a smart little girl, smarter than you think,'' Melina said softly. ''She probably knows more about the reasons behind your separation from her mother than you think she does. Small children aren't always able to explain the way they feel. As far as I can tell,'' Melina went on, ''Jamie is more worried I will supplant her in your life than she is by the divorce. You'll have to show her she'll always be number one in your life.''

Gazing at his new wife, Adam began to feel a

peace he hadn't felt for a long time. With Melina to help him understand the mind of a child, showing Jamie he loved her was going to be a piece of cake.

His pleasure lasted only until he remembered that one day Melina was bound to get her green card and drop out of their lives. What would that mean to Jamie?

And, now that he thought about it, what would it mean to him?

"I think I'll turn in," he said, rubbing his forehead. "I've got a headache that won't quit. Maybe things will look better after some shut-eye."

He paused and looked at Melina. "Sorry. I forgot you don't know all of our American expressions."

"No problem," Melina said airily. "To shut an eye means to sleep in any language, no?"

"No. I mean, yes," Adam laughed. "I think both of us could use a good night's sleep."

Melina uncurled herself from the couch and followed him to the bedroom. Knowing there was only one bed waiting for them, she was pretty sure neither she nor her convenient husband was likely to get much sleep tonight.

## Chapter Five

Adam was halfway into the bedroom before he realized he had a problem. Temptation was staring him in the face. Even if king-size, there was no way in hell that lone bed was going to be large enough for both him and Melina. Maybe for a couple of nights, but surely not for the entire time Jamie would spend with him.

Even bundling was out.

He'd learned that much from his experience in Corfu. The crowning moment had been when he'd awakened to find Melina running her fingers over his nude chest.

Surprised, but pleased, he'd been tempted to make the exploration mutual. It had only been her shocked reaction at finding him awake and willing that had abruptly cooled his libido.

He'd never been able to figure out the female mind. Not then, and not now.

After he'd realized bundling next to Melina without breaking his promise not to touch her wasn't going to work, remaining in Greece's most romantic island had become impossible. Faced with having to sleep in the same bed with Melina here in San Francisco for the next few weeks without touching was clearly going to be just as impossible. Not even with a mountain of pillows between them.

"I'm sorry," he said as he turned his back to the bed and tried to separate his mind from the call of his testosterone. "I clean forgot there are only two beds in the place and one of them is Jamie's."

Melina quirked an eyebrow. "How could you forget the three of us would be living together here?"

Adam shrugged. If she couldn't understand him, hell, he couldn't understand himself, either. He knew he looked foolish, but then he'd been behaving like a fool from the moment he'd first laid eyes on Melina. How else could he explain meeting and marrying a woman he'd never met before and in a space of three days? And overlooking the fact that it took two years for a woman married to an American citizen to get a green card.

A short week ago he'd been a conservative businessman with a largely satisfying lifestyle. Now, it was beginning to look as if he didn't know his left foot from his right, let alone have the ability to recall the accommodations of the place he called home.

"Everything has happened so fast," he said ruefully. "I'm lucky I can remember my name and address, let alone remember how many beds there are in here." He bit his lower lip and glanced back at the living room. "I guess I *could* sleep on the couch."

"No! What if Jamie happens to wake up and finds you there? She may be only six, but she's old enough to have noticed that husbands and wives sleep together," Melina protested. "You can't possibly risk her asking why you're sleeping on the couch instead of here in bed with me."

"You're right, the couch is out." Adam glared at the bed as if it was responsible for his problem. He raked his hand through his hair and wandered back into the living room. Perhaps if he put an armchair and a hassock together he could create a bed, but he'd be damned if he was going to sleep curled up like a pretzel for the next few months. "We'll just have to try to come up with something."

"Something? What is this something?"

"Bundling," he said as he kept a wary eye on her. "I know it didn't work before, but this time it's going to be for real."

Melina tried to look innocent. If he was thinking about her sexual reaction to him in Corfu, so was she. Telling Adam or herself that she'd only been dreaming when she'd awakened him by exploring the muscles on his chest wasn't the whole truth. She *had* wanted to touch him. She had wanted him to touch her. If they did decide to bundle, the biggest thing she had to worry about was herself.

She smothered a sigh. Adam might be trying to hide the way he looked at her, but she'd be foolish to read anything romantic into that look. She hadn't had much experience on the subject, but she recognized a look of desire; a pure and simple look of lust.

He'd made himself clear from the beginning that their impulsive marriage was only for convenience. And wasn't their agreement clear that the marriage would only last for the time it took her to get her green card? Surely, Jamie would be out of the picture before then. To expect anything more would be asking for the moon, only to find it was made of green cheese.

On the other hand, she mused as she gazed at the bed, she might be an inexperienced virgin, but she'd learned enough from her experience in Corfu to know bundling didn't work. Her only excuse was that, virgin or not, bundling or not, spending the night in the same bed with a man like Adam was enough to tempt any woman, even in her sleep.

''This ought to do it, at least for tonight,'' Adam said as he returned with an armload of pillows. ''If this doesn't work—'' he eyed the bed with a grim look ''—we'll have to play it by ear.''

''That's okay. I'll stay awake all night to make sure this bundling works this time.''

''No way,'' Adam said as he dropped the pillows onto the bed. ''If anyone is going to make sure this is going to work, it's going to be me. I'll stay awake.'' He eyed her for a long moment until a heat began to work its way through her middle. A reminder that it had been she who had made the first move.

Melina gathered her vanity case and headed for the bathroom. She seemed to have no control over the way she felt about Adam, awake or asleep.

With Adam obviously determined to honor their no-touching-in-private agreement, she was wasting any sensual thoughts. Wide awake, in spite of the symptoms of jet lag that should have sent her to sleep, she tried to find something else to think about besides sleeping with Adam. Virgin she might be, but wanton she was not, she told herself firmly. At least, when she was awake.

She was back in fifteen minutes dressed in the pink bridal nightgown and matching robe Eleni had given her for a wedding present.

Adam blinked when Melina reappeared looking like a bride and smelling of scented soap. Her nightgown, at least the part showing through her sheer robe, was held up by slender straps, gathered under her breasts and barely came to her knees. Her short, curly, dark hair was held off her face with a matching pink ribbon, but a few damp curls had managed to escape. Her long, slender legs ended with those ten bewitching manicured toes.

Adam groaned. Intentional or not, the look in her almond-shaped Mediterranean eyes was an invitation. He took a deep breath and tried to remember theirs wasn't a real marriage. But real or not, Adam's body stirred and his mind began to spin. How in heaven's name was he going to be able to spend the next few weeks hiding behind a barrier of pillows? Or, if worse came to worst, sleeping on the floor?

He bit back a string of curses. No way had he bargained for this, he told himself as he avoided meeting Melina's eyes. He busied himself by rummaging in a dresser drawer for something to wear to bed tonight. Normally, unless Jamie was with him, he slept in the raw, but not tonight. And definitely not now with the emotions he was beginning to feel for Melina.

As long as they remained together, there had to be a way he could convince her to wear flannel nightgowns. Long nightgowns buttoned from her slender throat to those manicured toes, sleeves that came to her wrists, and loose enough so he wouldn't be tempted to even visualize her lush body.

No way had he even stopped to think of the possibility that he might fall for his convenient bride, he thought ruefully. Instead here he was falling faster than a nonstop elevator dropping fifty floors.

Fat chance. There was nothing and everything about Melina that didn't ring his bell.

From what Peter had told him about the fire in Greek women, he shouldn't have been surprised by the way Melina looked. Either the Greek men Melina had come into contact with had been blind or her traditional father had managed to scare them away. After having met Kostos and seen the man in action, he still had to sympathize with him. No wonder the man had been finally driven to ordering her to find a husband or threatening to find one for her.

His thoughts turned to his own daughter. If this was what the future held, he'd have to find a nunnery to keep Jamie safe until the right man came along.

"This ought to do the trick." Adam gestured to the barrier of pillows. "I'll be back as soon as I check on Jamie and shower."

Afraid she might fall asleep and act out a dream again, Melina got into bed, pulled the blankets up to her chin and forced herself to stay awake until Adam reappeared.

When he came out of the bathroom, he was stripped to his boxers and a skimpy T-shirt that barely covered his chest and shoulders. Drops of shower water clung to his hair. Avoiding Melina's gaze, he climbed into the other side of the barrier and turned his back to her. "I'm sure beat," he said over his shoulder. "We'll talk more about this in the morning. Good night."

*"Kallinixta, Adam,"* Melina called softly. "Good night," she repeated softly when he lapsed into silence.

It was strange the way she reverted to her native language when her thoughts turned to Adam. But Melina wasn't really surprised; no other man had ever stirred her the way Adam did. Adam might be able to fall asleep, but as for her, sleep was out. Not with Adam on the other side of the pillow barrier, and not when the barrier seemed to be closing in on her. And definitely not when she was afraid to doze off for fear of what she might do in her sleep.

She couldn't see Adam's face, but between the sounds of muttered curses and the way he threw himself against his pillow, she knew he was just as uneasy about being in bed together as she was. Maybe it was because he knew he'd fraudulently vowed to love, honor and cherish her. In her own heart, the vows had been truly made. Tonight, she felt like a wife in bed with her new husband. The more Adam tossed, the more sinful her thoughts became.

She turned onto her side and eyed the mountain of pillows that separated them.

Desire told her that, after all, they *were* married and if a pillow or two should happen to become dislodged, it wouldn't be a crime. But, her conscience reminded her the marriage was only a charade for the benefit of the United States Immigration authorities.

Common sense told her this was no time to give up the dubious honor of being the last twenty-nine-year-old virgin in Greece, and maybe, although she doubted it, in the entire United States.

Her mind wandered. As far as she knew, there were no backward small villages like Nafplion in this liberated American society. Or any old-fashioned and suspicious fathers like hers. This was, after all, the twenty-first century. Maybe not in her village back home in Greece, but definitely here.

Her thoughts turned to how it would feel to be held in Adam's arms, to feel his lips brushing her breasts, to hear his whispered sweet words of endearment in her ear. To share all the pent-up longing churning inside for someone of her own to love and to cherish. To honor the vows she'd made to Adam.

"This is *not* going to work!" she finally heard Adam mutter. One more violent turn and the pillow barrier collapsed. She found herself head to head and eye to eye with the man she ached to touch, the man she wanted to make love to her.

And this time, it was no dream. Not when his eyes narrowed as they roamed over her. She held her breath, afraid to invite him to hold her. After a pause he clicked on the bed lamp and leaned over her.

"Sorry about this," he muttered. His voice trailed off before he began again. "That is, I didn't mean to…" He gestured to the flattened barrier.

*"Tipota."* She smiled at the look of frustration on Adam's face. "Nothing. Think nothing of it," she said in English, although he knew what she'd meant. "I was awake. I haven't been able to sleep, either."

Adam pushed away what was left of the pillow barrier, leaned on one elbow and regarded her in a way that made her senses whirl. "Believe it or not," he began, "it's been a while since I've been interested in pillow talk, but this is different. Truthfully, I've been wishing we knew each other better."

"Pillow talk?" Melina's heart turned a somersault when she realized her mother's wisdom about cementing a marriage could be coming true. Adam had to be signaling she meant more to him than a mere marriage-of-convenience bride. At least he was acting like a friend, if not a new husband.

She settled back against the pillows. "What did you want to know about me?"

"You don't have to answer, if you don't want to…" he said slowly, "but I was wondering why you haven't gotten married by now."

"You could say I never found a man I could love."

"So you decided to look around in a new country for a husband?"

"No," she said softly, reluctant to tell him she'd already found the man she wanted for a husband.

How could she tell him men had desired her for most of her adult life? That if she'd simply wanted sex, she could have had it anytime. If she'd simply wanted marriage, she would have obeyed her father and married the man of his choice. What she did want was for Adam to love her, not just to lust after her.

Gazing at the longing in Adam's eyes, it would have been easy to tell him how she felt. She couldn't, not without the chance she might give in to that longing. She'd managed to maintain her virginity for almost twenty-nine years only because her self-respect meant more to her than momentary satisfaction.

Adam was gazing at her in a way that made her hormones squirm. If this kept up, she was afraid she'd find herself in his arms. She glanced at the travel clock Adam had put on the nightstand. "Maybe we should try to sleep?"

"After spending sixteen hours in the air, you'd think we would be tired enough," Adam said with a glance at the clock. He sighed. "Tomorrow morning isn't that far away."

At Melina's fleeting look of disappointment, he started to reach for her. He wanted to bury his lips in her breasts, to find out if she tasted as soft and as sweet as she looked.

He hesitated when he realized the warm look in her almond-shaped eyes could turn a man into a cinder and take him down paths he knew he should avoid. Then, too, she'd only believe he was taking unfair advantage of her vulnerability, he told himself. He'd promised not to touch her in private, so what was he thinking of? He'd never broken a promise in his life, and he didn't intend to start now.

"Melina," he said softly as he reluctantly pulled away. "I'm sorry. I honestly meant to keep our agreement, but...it's just that there's something about you that gets to me.

"If only..." he went on before, frustrated by his mixed emotions, he shook his head. "Maybe we should have thought this whole thing out more carefully before we rushed into this marriage. It's not fair to you."

Melina thought back to his unexpected marriage

proposal. A proposal he'd appeared to regret as soon as he'd made it. Just as it sounded as if he regretted it now.

"I thought I knew what I was doing by accepting your marriage proposal. Now," she said slowly, "I'm not so sure. I realize that this arrangement can't be fair to you, either. You might find someone you really want to marry someday."

A rueful smile curved at Adam's lips. "No, thanks. As for this—" he gestured to the pillow barrier "—I won't pretend sleeping this way will be easy, but I'll try to manage."

"Me, too," she said softly. So softly he wasn't sure he'd heard what she'd said. He eyed her with a rueful grin.

"Maybe we can bend the no-touching rule for tonight? Just long enough for a kiss of friendship so we can both go to sleep?" he said as he outlined her bottom lip with a gentle forefinger. "What do you say?"

Mesmerized by the sensuous look in Adam's eyes, Melina leaned toward him. *"Thelo na se fileeso,"* she said softly, gambling he wouldn't know that she was saying, *I want to kiss you too.* "Just a kiss to help us sleep," she said as she moved closer to him. "We will let tomorrow take care of itself, yes?"

"Yes." He leaned over, cradled her head in his hands and bent to kiss her.

"Daddy! Daddy!" Jamie's frantic voice suddenly broke into the sexual tension. "There's a monster in my room!"

Adam's body cooled at the sound of abject terror in his daughter's voice. He took a deep breath, threw back the covers and jumped out of bed. "I'm sorry," he said with an apologetic look over his shoulder before he dashed out of the bedroom. "I'm coming, sweetheart!" he shouted. "Daddy's coming!"

Her body aching for Adam's kiss, his touch, Melina fell back against her pillow with a sigh. She couldn't blame him. He was a father, and his daughter came first. For that matter, she thought ruefully as she tried to find a place for herself, all parents must go through unsatisfied moments like these.

She would do well to remember she had been hired on to be Jamie's nanny. Not as Adam's real wife.

WOUND UP tighter than a clock, his mind back in the other bedroom with Melina, Adam comforted his frightened little daughter until she fell asleep. Poor darling, she had so many changes in her short life, no wonder she dreamed of monsters.

Maybe it was just as well Jamie had called to him

before it was too late. Only now he had demons of his own to confront. The last few minutes with Melina in bed beside him had been sheer torture. Heaven help him, he'd been on the verge of satisfying the hunger he'd seen in her eyes and the hunger he'd felt for her. He'd yearned to satisfy that unexpected undeniable hunger, and not only because she was a desirable woman.

Somewhere along the line, he'd been struck by the tender understanding she'd shown even after he'd behaved like an ass.

He sensed she would have given him the kiss they both longed for. If he did go back and take up where he'd left off, he'd only be adding to the problems that kept them apart. He might even wind up with a wife who didn't want him for a husband. She might wind up with a husband and stepdaughter when all she wanted was her freedom. If he was smart, he thought as he absentmindedly smoothed Jamie's hair where the scent of powdered sugar still clung, he'd stay right where he was until Melina fell asleep. At least until he'd cooled down enough to keep his distance from his too-convenient wife.

MELINA AWAKENED with a start and realized she'd fallen asleep while waiting for Adam to return. She opened her eyes to the first gray-yellow rays of dawn that had found their way between the thin white plastic bedroom shutters and listened for sounds of someone stirring.

Disappointed at the way the night had ended, she eyed the empty half of the bed where Adam's pillow still carried the dent of his head. The pillows that had made up the barrier were scattered helter-skelter on the bed.

Love comes when you least expect it, she mused. This time love had come with a price. She bargained for a loveless marriage, but to her surprise the agreement had changed.

She scrambled across the bed on her knees and peered over Adam's side of the bed. True to his word, Adam was asleep on his back on the carpeted floor. Not only asleep, he was fully dressed and, clearly uneasy, muttering in his sleep.

She leaned closer to hear what he was saying. All she could make out were the occasional words of ''can't'' and ''sorry,'' as if he was apologizing. To her? Was that why he'd dressed before he'd come back to sleep? To make sure there would no temptation?

Melina leaned back on an oversize pillow and sighed. If Adam were really tormented by their close quarters and their clearly mutual attraction, she'd have to do her part to help him. She had to try harder to ensure their desire remained unconsummated. If she had to keep her distance, she would. Not only for his sake, but for hers. She couldn't afford to have her heart broken.

She sighed, leaned over the side of the bed and blew the sleeping man a kiss. "Sleep well, my love."

No more sheer nightgowns, she decided as she tried to sleep. They might give Adam the wrong impression. As for the rest of her clothing, she had a few dresses in her suitcases from her position at the American embassy that made her look dowdy and unappealing. Dresses she'd worn because she hadn't been sure of herself. She'd never given herself the chance to find the right man until she'd been terminated and Adam had come along. A pity, she thought as she settled back in bed and tried to forget that Adam was only a few feet away.

She finally drifted off to an uneasy sleep thinking that now that she'd found a man she knew she could fall in love with, he'd turned out to be the wrong man for her.

## Chapter Six

The next morning Melina was in the kitchen preparing breakfast when Adam made his appearance.
Freshly showered, the scent of his bay rum shaving
lotion clung to him.

Today, instead of a business suit, he was wearing
casual tan slacks and a brown-and-white-checked,
open-neck shirt. The colors set off his hazel eyes
and the gold tones in his brown hair. Melina's heart
skipped.

"Good morning," she murmured, embarrassed to
meet his matter-of-fact gaze. How could he appear
so nonchalant after their close encounter last night?

"Good morning." Adam came into the kitchen
and sniffed appreciatively at the scent of the warm
sweet rolls she'd just taken out of the oven. "Looks
like you've managed to keep busy."

Melina tried focusing on icing the rolls instead of
on the damp curls she glimpsed on Adam's chest. If

he could behave as if nothing unusual had happened last night, so could she, but it wasn't easy. "I'm afraid I'm still on Athens time. Since I couldn't fall back to sleep, I decided to make breakfast."

She didn't explain that what had kept her awake most of the night had been the sensuous look in Adam's eyes just before he'd leaned over and lowered his lips to meet hers. Considering what had happened next, or rather, hadn't happened, she couldn't tell him how much she'd longed for that kiss. Or that she longed for it now.

A warning voice inside her mind told her that she was playing with fire, but surely a single kiss wouldn't have made a difference?

The problem had been that she'd already made up her mind to give up the dubious honor of being a twenty-nine-going-on-thirty-year-old virgin. Now that she and Adam were married, she'd chosen him to initiate her into lovemaking. More importantly, she was on the verge of falling in love with him.

It had only been Jamie's calling out to her father that had kept her from falling into his arms.

Better to keep the secret of how desirable she found him, she thought with an inward sigh. If she needed further proof he'd thought the impulse to kiss her had been a mistake, after he'd calmed Jamie, he'd spent the rest of the night sleeping on the floor instead of coming back to her. And taking up where he'd left off.

She bit back another sigh at her wayward thoughts. Back in Athens, they'd made a bargain to have a marriage of convenience. If Adam was trying to honor their agreement, could she do any less?

Adam watched as Melina carefully spread white icing across the warm rolls. To his bemusement, she ran the tip of her tongue across her lips to catch a tiny drop of icing. Instinctively his body stirred. In another time and in another circumstance, he would have wiped the icing off with his lips. Too bad they'd decided she was off limits.

What was there about the woman that made his senses spin whenever he looked into those enchanting lavender, Mediterranean eyes? How in heaven's name was he going to be able to live with her for the next few months and still keep from making her his wife for real?

The idea they could manage a real marriage was ridiculous. No matter how intense the physical attraction between them, their hopes, dreams and plans were as far apart as the cities of Athens and San Francisco. He didn't need, or, for that matter, *want* another permanent relationship to frustrate him. Not when he'd already learned, courtesy of his ex-wife, that no woman wanted an on-again, off-again husband.

No way was he going to go near Melina today, let alone sleep in the same bed with her tonight. Last night's miss had been a warning call even though she had made his body stir.

Adam was about to turn away before Melina could see his body's reaction to her, when he realized he might be wrong in avoiding the truth. Worrying about the future was one thing. His sexual reaction to having Melina in bed with him was another. Better to apologize for his adolescent behavior last night than to leave a sexual tension hanging between them. He'd started to apologize to her when he heard Jamie's voice.

"Daddy! I'm up!" Wearing a short pink nightgown covered with white teddy bears running across the hem, Jamie burst into the kitchen. She skidded to a stop when she spotted Melina spreading icing across the sweet rolls. "Oh, goody. Can I lick the spoon?"

"Just as soon as you get dressed," Melina answered with a laugh. "If you like, then you can have a sweet roll and a glass of milk for breakfast."

"No cereal?" Jamie asked cautiously. "Are you sure? Mommy says cereal makes me grow."

"You're right. Cereal does make you grow, but you don't have to grow anymore today," Melina said with a smile. "Today is special. Even your father is staying home."

''Wow!'' Jamie twirled on tiny toes, blew a kiss to her father and headed back to her bedroom. ''I'll be right back!''

The scene was so moving, so natural, that Adam's thoughts turned to the past. He'd never taken a day off unless he'd been sick. If he had spent more time with his family, and he and his ex-wife had stayed together, would Jamie have been better off?

He wished he could go back six years to begin all over again. He'd had to travel on business, yes, but he could have taken his wife and child with him.

Too bad he hadn't had the twenty-twenty vision back then that he had today. The same vision told him, given the opportunity, Melina was the type of woman who could provide the family he'd longed for and had so casually given up.

A sudden rush of feeling had caught him by surprise as he'd gazed at the interaction between Melina and Jamie. He'd been stunned. He'd never thought his emotions would get away from him this way, but they'd been in a turmoil ever since he'd first laid eyes on her.

There wasn't anything he could do about it now, he thought as he cleared his throat. He'd impulsively made his pact with Melina and that was that. He hadn't reckoned on falling for her, nor had he stopped to think of the possible consequences if he had. He was an honorable man, he told his aching body. Not only was an agreement an agreement, he didn't need the future problem of losing another wife. If he consummated the marriage and Melina still wanted to leave as soon as she qualified for a green card, they'd both be hurt.

"Would you like something hot to drink with the rolls?" Melina asked. "Coffee?"

"Ah, the thick, strong Greek coffee that looks like mud and puts hair on my chest?" Adam sauntered over and looked down at the oddly shaped little brass Greek coffeemaker she had in her hand. "Yes, please," he said, relieved at the change in the atmosphere. Sensual musing had its time and place and this wasn't it. "I got hooked on it the first time I visited Athens."

"Thick as mud? Hair on your chest?" Melina paused in measuring out the finely ground aromatic Greek coffee. This morning, of all mornings, the reference to the hair on his chest was the last thing she needed to hear. Not when it brought back memories of her impulsive exploration of his chest in Corfu. And of her misplaced fascination with him now.

"That was just another saying. Don't let it bother you." Adam laughed and reached around her for a sweet roll cooling on the counter. "I guess I'll have to remember not to use odd American expressions around you."

Melina blushed when Adam's hand brushed the

side of her breast in passing. She raised her eyes to meet Adam's and caught a glimpse of a rueful smile. Instinctively she sensed he was thinking of something more than the night in Corfu. He had to be remembering last night.

Her middle warmed as she realized there had to be more to Adam's embarrassment than the aborted kiss. He'd been in and out of Greece often enough to have understood some of the words of endearment she'd murmured to the back of his head last night.

Melina hesitantly returned Adam's smile, then busied herself stirring and pouring the coffee. She'd never considered Greek coffee as lava, she thought as she gazed at the movement of the thick liquid. The strong and bitter coffee did resemble the sensuous flow of molten lava, but she'd never before related it to the sexual movements between a man and a woman.

She did now.

She gestured to a chair to cover her confusion. "If you would sit, I'll have your breakfast in a few minutes."

"Sure," Adam said as he eyed the plate of freshly baked sweet rolls. "I never expected anything like this." He smiled at her. "I'm a lucky guy. You're great with children and you're a great baker! What else are you good at?"

Adam realized the possible sexual connotation behind the question as soon as the question left his lips. Melina's eyes lit up, a mischievous smile hovering at her lips. The first real smile he'd seen all morning.

"As a woman?" she asked with a sexy glance that shook him down to his toes.

Adam's eyes widened as he realized she'd been referring to the only kiss they'd exchanged since the day they'd met; at their wedding.

"That too," Adam said with a careless shrug, even as he felt his body tighten and his senses stir. If she only knew how he did relate to her as a man relates to a desirable woman, she'd grab her things and take the first flight back to Athens. He'd be wise to remember she'd only agreed to be a nanny.

*Love does indeed come when you least expect it.* Melina realized again as she marveled at the way Adam's hazel eyes darkened. Too bad her growing attraction for him wasn't shared. If it had been, he wouldn't be talking about child care, baking, and asking meaningless questions. His arms would be wrapped around her, his kisses a prelude to the closeness she longed for.

Would Adam have made love to her last night if she'd told him she had been and was still willing?

Perhaps it was just as well Jamie had interrupted them last night. Maybe Adam's physical reaction to finding the pillow barrier between them gone was only what every red-blooded man would have felt at finding a willing woman in bed with him. Especially since they'd already exchanged marriage vows.

"All Greek women know how to cook," she finally answered with a shrug that belied the way her heart was beating wildly. "That's only one of the reasons we make such good wives."

"And the other reasons?" He couldn't help himself.

She took a deep breath. "I'm told we have a fire inside of us."

Adam raised an eyebrow and saluted her with a half-eaten sweet roll. "Here's to that fire!"

Melina acknowledged the salute, but since she had no wish to force an obviously reluctant Adam into acknowledging her as a desirable woman, she turned away. Still, she thought as she served him a bowl of sliced ripe peaches and another fragrant roll, it was easy to imagine a night of passion with him. And afterward, long afterward, an intimate breakfast.

She pondered the personality of the man who was her "husband." She knew by now Adam was normally a pragmatic man who planned ahead and disliked leaving anything to chance. She also knew from the bits of information he'd dropped the last few days that his long-range plans didn't include a wife.

She would have to be careful not to try to push him into a false marriage or she'd never forgive herself.

"Is there a problem? Something I said?" Adam asked when she silently sipped her coffee.

Melina started at the sound of his voice. The problem wasn't what he'd said. It was what he hadn't said. She'd given him a perfect opening with her comment about the fire within her to pursue their unusual relationship and he'd made a joke out of it. "What makes you think so?"

He took a sip of hot coffee. "Sorry, maybe I don't have the right to intrude into your thoughts. But," he went on in a rush, "if you're thinking about that, er..." He flushed and started over. "I just wanted you to know that last night was never going to turn into more than a kiss. Just a kiss. By the way," he added quickly before she could comment, "I've come up with a solution to our sleeping arrangements. I'm going to rent a couch that opens into a bed...a sofa bed. Of course," he added with a glance at the door to Jamie's bedroom, "it means we still have to sleep in the same room."

"So that no one will ever know the truth?"

"For now. I think we should at least sleep in the same room in case Jamie notices and begins to wonder about us. And in case the INS comes snooping. You don't mind, do you?''

''Not at all, although last night meant nothing,'' Melina said casually, even though she knew it wasn't true. She'd wanted Adam as much as he'd seemed to want her, but for different reasons. He seemed to want her because of their proximity. She wanted him because of her growing attraction for him.

''A couch will be fine.'' She tried to match his pragmatic tone. ''Although I think I should be the one to sleep on the couch. I'm much shorter than you are.'' She poured coffee for herself and, without meeting Adam's gaze, joined him at the table. He must know he didn't have to take all the blame for the near embrace last night. He must have known she had been willing.

He made no mention of his spending most of the night sleeping on the floor, although he had to know she'd seen him there in the morning.

She knew the reason without asking. Just as she'd known why he hadn't come back to bed after Jamie had gone to sleep. It had been a sure way to keep himself from picking up where he'd left off before he'd been interrupted.

Then, too, maybe he was thinking about her role in Jamie's life. Maybe he was trying to make it clear he considered her his daughter's nanny, nothing more.

If that was his only reason, she could even understand that one. A favorite of her own father as a little girl, Melina knew a little girl deserved all the attention her father could give her.

"What do you say we go downtown and apply for your green card this morning? Maybe with a little sight-seeing afterward. You don't want to lose any time."

Adam's question, while not unexpected, was like a splash of ice-cold water. Sure, she'd wanted a green card, but she realized she wanted to be Adam's wife even more.

Foolish woman, she thought. Here she'd been melting inside, thinking of the way Adam had gazed at her, while he was wondering how soon he could be rid of her.

"That would be nice," Melina replied as she reluctantly put the thought of the possibility of someday becoming Adam's true wife behind her. "We can take Jamie with us." She paused and pushed her unfinished cup of coffee away. "Before we go, I wish you would think more about my taking care of Jamie even while you're here. She has to become used to me, sooner or later."

"That is a problem," Adam agreed reluctantly. "I should have stopped to consider the possible effect on her before I asked you to marry me. As it is, she's not happy about us. I'm afraid things will be more difficult for her if she comes to care for you and you eventually leave.''

*One more reason not to allow his little girl, and himself, not to become involved with her.* How many reasons would Adam come up with in an attempt to keep his distance?

''A nanny is one thing, a stepmother is another,'' Melina said soberly. ''I will tell Jamie the truth. I can explain as gently as I know how that I am only here until I get my green card or until she returns to her mother.''

''No!'' Adam exploded. ''The whole crazy idea of a marriage of convenience was stupid and it's my responsibility to handle any fallout.'' He bit back his frustration. ''I'm sorry, Melina, but the truth is, I never intended to go through with the offer of marriage. I told you that before, but what you don't know is that it wasn't until your father assumed I'd compromised you that I couldn't let you face the consequences alone. I decided not to try to back out of my proposal, not then and not now. I'm also man enough to be able to explain the truth to my daughter.''

*The truth?* Shocked at Adam's reluctant confession that he had never intended to go through with the marriage of convenience until her father inferred

Adam had taken her virginity, Melina's dreams shattered. She'd known Adam's offer had been impulsive, but she'd never really listened to her father's accusation. Nor had she realized the reason Adam had felt compelled to go through with the marriage.

She'd been a fool to dream of a future with Adam, and a bigger fool to think that someday after they'd gotten to know each other, the dream would come true.

Adam called his confession the whole truth. He'd been wrong. The real whole truth was that he regretted his offer.

Melina silently gathered up the used cups and plates and carried them to the sink. Adam couldn't have been more clear. He couldn't wait to rid himself of her. Any idea she might have entertained to try to broach the distance between them died a quick death. From now on, she vowed as she rinsed and stacked the cups and plates in the dishwasher, she would fill the job she'd been hired for, and nothing more. Jamie's nanny.

"TWO YEARS?"

"That's what I was told." Adam gazed ruefully at the sheaf of papers the clerk in the INS office had given him. "And that's only from the time we hand in the completed forms and the authorities have a chance to investigate. Lord knows how long that will take. Seems there's a rush to get in under the newest deadline for applying for a green card.''

Melina gazed at the stack of forms Adam held in his hand. The number of people lined up inside the Immigration and Naturalization Service office applying for the right to live in and work in the United States had been an indicator that her chances of getting the green card anytime soon was impossible.

''Is there no other way I can get the card?''

''I'm afraid not,'' Adam replied. ''Not in these times, and not without a lawyer.'' He gazed at the long lines in the office and back to Melina. ''You're sure you want to go through with this? Maybe you'd rather go home?''

She shook her head. ''I'm sure. I love my country, but I've dreamed for years of coming to the United States. I've dreamed of being free to live as I choose,'' she added, gazing at Adam through unshed tears. ''I have only been in your country for two days, but I already know I will love living here.''

''Melina…'' Adam said uneasily, ''why don't we take this outside?''

Melina nodded in agreement.

Once outside the INS office, Adam continued, ''I've told you that the offer I made you about coming here started as an impulse. Maybe your taking me up on it was an impulse, too.'' He hesitated and stopped to check on Jamie. Thankfully she was investigating a vending machine a few feet away. "Considering our present circumstances, I'm sure we can get an annulment. You'll be free to go home to Greece anytime you want to."

He felt like a heel when he saw a blush cover Melina's face at the reminder they hadn't consummated their marriage. "I'm sorry. I didn't mean to embarrass you. The plain truth is that since we haven't…" His voice trailed off. "What I meant to say…" he began again. "It wouldn't take much to free you from our marriage."

"And what of Jamie? What of my promise to take care of her?"

"I'll take care of her. Now that I'm home again, I'll make arrangements to stick around for a few months. I'm sure I'll be able to find someone to take care of her now that I'm here."

"No," Melina said proudly. "I made a promise and I intend to keep it, with or without a green card." She didn't add that, even if he chose to ignore it, she'd also made a promise to love, honor and cherish him and intended to keep it.

"Now that you've met my father," she went on, "you must realize if I go home he will only believe I realized I made a mistake and have come home to repent. He would insist I marry a man of his choice. I would be expected to remain in Nafplion with my husband. I couldn't bear it."

"Maybe not. Maybe your father might just lose his temper. He loves you enough to let you choose your own husband."

"Of course he loves me," Melina sighed. "I love him, too. But he is my father. He believes it is his duty to see to my future, my happiness. You must understand that my parents' marriage was arranged by their parents, and that their marriage has been a happy one. He has always said love comes after a marriage, and he is old-fashioned enough to believe it."

"Daddy!" Jamie's voice broke in. "I'm hungry. Can I have a candy bar?"

Troubled by Melina's obvious unhappiness, Adam put the forms under his arm and reached into his pocket for change. "Hang on. I'll be there in a minute! We'll talk later about this," he quietly told Melina.

Melina shook her head, then reached to stay his hand. "No!"

"No?" Adam looked surprised. "I thought we were going to decide on what to do about you."

"Not me, Jamie. I meant you shouldn't let Jamie have candy. She's had a sweet roll and milk for breakfast. She needs to have a balanced lunch—no more sugar."

Jamie looked back over her shoulder. "Daddy?"

Adam hesitated for a moment, then nodded his

agreement. "Not now, sweetheart. You need to have a decent lunch. How about showing Melina Fisherman's Wharf? We can have our lunch there."

Jamie set up a howl. Adam remained firm. "Lunch." He reached for Jamie's arm. "Lunch. Come on, I know you like eating at the wharf."

"Not now. Today I'm hungry for a chocolate bar." Jamie glared at Melina. "It's all your fault, I know it is!"

"Jamie! Mind your manners!" Adam scolded. He'd always been too soft on his daughter, but as a part-time father, he hadn't been able to help it. He didn't have her often enough to be strict about her eating habits, or, for that matter, anything else.

"Melina is right, and so am I. Her rules are my rules. You need to eat something healthy for lunch."

Jamie pouted and hung back. "I want to go home to my mommy."

Melina motioned Adam aside and crouched in front of Jamie. "Remember how you told me your mother insisted on a healthy breakfast every morning?"

Jamie stuck out her lower lip.

Melina knew that if she were to make any headway in their tenuous relationship, it would have to be by continuing to invoke Jamie's mother's name. "You had something sweet for breakfast, dear." She repeated. "I am sure your mother would be happier if you had a good lunch."

Adam stood silently, taken by Melina's patience even when faced with a child who resented her. Anyone else wouldn't have wasted time setting his daughter straight.

It was his fault, Adam thought in despair. When Jamie was with him, seldom as it may have been, her visits had been a whatever-she'd-wanted ball game. Out of respect for Jamie's mother, and out of his love for his little girl, he realized now there should have been rules to follow. For everyone's good.

It looked as if Melina was here to stay for a little while, thank God. At least for the two years it could take for her to get a green card. He would have to do something to show both Melina and Jamie he considered them his family. There would be no favorites, no skirting of rules and no backing out on promises.

And that included the promises he'd made to Melina.

## Chapter Seven

Adam, none too thrilled at the prospect of having to sleep apart, knowing himself too well to even try lying with Melina again, had ordered a sofa bed before they'd left the house for the day.

The sight-seeing tour passed pleasantly. To his relief, Jamie was finally too tired to act up. By the time they returned from lunch and sight-seeing at Fisherman's Wharf, the deliverymen were waiting outside Adam's hillside town house. From the jaundiced looks the men were giving him, it was clear they weren't too happy about having had to wait. The prospect of wrestling the sofa up a flight of stairs didn't improve their moods.

Adam dubiously eyed the monstrous piece of furniture. He'd ordered the largest sleep sofa available, but it didn't take a genius to realize that, big as it was, the sofa bed wasn't going to be long enough to accommodate him. Smothering a sigh, he led the way upstairs.

Melina settled Jamie in the living room with a glass of milk and a plate of cookies to watch her favorite cartoons. A promise of a manicure after Jamie's bath helped.

As soon as the deliverymen left with an ample reward for their efforts, Melina joined Adam in the bedroom, where he stood regarding his new bed. "Are you sure you'll fit in there?"

Adam shrugged as he gazed dubiously at the sofa bed. "I have to. It's a little short, but it's got to be better than sleeping on the floor."

"The sofa is not long enough for you." Melina said firmly, with a glance over her shoulder to make sure Jamie was still engrossed in her movie. "I will sleep there. You take the bed."

Adam gazed at her for a watchful moment before he carefully closed the bedroom door and came back to join her. How could he tell her he'd rented the sofa bed largely for her sake? That he knew damn well that he wouldn't be able to keep from wanting his arms around her, finally making her his?

How to tell Melina he was beginning to care for her in ways that continued to puzzle him? That he'd begun to change without realizing it.

He had to do something, and now. He recalled the old saying that nothing ventured was nothing gained—he had to take a last chance at connecting with her. "I'm willing to take the bed, Melina," he offered with his fingers mentally crossed, "but only if you share it with me. If you're willing, we can go back to bundling."

Melina gazed at the bed. "I thought you said bundling wasn't working. That *is* why you slept on the floor last night, no?"

"Yes," he said with hope in his heart. At least she hadn't said no. "The floor was too damn hard. I only slept there last night because I knew I couldn't sleep in the same bed with you without touching you."

Melina blushed.

"I want you," Adam went on frankly, "and not just because you're a desirable woman, Melina. The truth is, I'm beginning to care for you." He went on, surprised at his thoughts. "I've realized you're everything I ever wanted in a woman."

A wave of warmth began to spread through her as she gazed at the frankly sensuous way Adam was regarding her. "I thought you were trying to keep this a marriage of convenience."

Adam shrugged helplessly. "I thought so, too, until now. But that doesn't change the way I've begun to feel about you. You're a wonderful woman. Intriguing and, if you don't mind my saying so," he added with a wicked grin, "very sexy."

Melina blushed. "You can't know for sure. We only met a short time ago."

"I know enough," he answered. "I'd like a chance to show you how much. On the other hand…" he added at the hesitancy he saw in Melina's eyes. He had to give her a choice. He had to stop pressuring her. "Considering I've agreed to your no-touching agreement, maybe it *would* be wrong if we did sleep together?" He brushed her cheek with the back of his hand, searched her warm lavender eyes and asked the question only she could answer. "Or would it?"

Adam's gaze bore into hers as if he were trying to read her very soul. He was trying to declare affection for her and, manlike, finding it hard to do. Virgin or not, she wanted him enough to help him tell her so.

Melina caught his hand in hers and carried it to her lips. "I am glad you feel free enough to tell me how you feel, Adam *mou*. I feel the same way about you," she said as she felt herself ache with her longing for him. "I wish more than anything to have you make love to me."

Adam's eyes lit up. He took a step toward her, with a glance at the closed door. "Now?" he said in a voice that sent shivers down Melina's spine.

Melina backed away. "No. Even though we are man and wife, we are still strangers. What if this attraction between us turns out to be nothing more than physical desire?"

"I'm afraid I'm not thinking of tomorrow." Adam pulled her closer, so close his body heat set her on fire. "I can't believe it's wrong for us to feel this way. This is the twenty-first century. We're not children."

"No, I am not a child." She smiled impishly at him. "It is not wrong to want to love. It is very good. I am just afraid this is not the right time and the right place—" her hand swept the bedroom "—to make such decisions. First, we need to talk and to get to know each other."

"Talk?" Adam regarded her with a wry grin. "Just like a woman. I've told you everything you need to know about me. What else could there possibly be to talk about?"

"It's not only that," Melina said as she tried to move away from the temptation of his curving mouth. "What I am saying is, that when I give myself to a man, I wish to give myself to the man I can spend the rest of my life with. If you will forgive me, Adam, I am not yet sure *you* think you are that man." She left unsaid that she considered him to be that man.

Adam wasn't sure he was that man, either. He reluctantly let her go and opened the bedroom door. "Okay. We'll do this your way. I'll sleep on the sofa bed tonight. It might take time, but I intend to show you how much I want you.''

Melina's longing to be loved by her husband-in-name-only started to fade. Adam might want her as she wanted him, but it was for all the wrong reasons. He hadn't said he loved her. Would he want her in his life after she obtained the green card?

Did he want to start a family with her? The family she'd dreamed about for years?

She had to hold back from rushing into his arms until she had the answers to those questions.

She would have to school herself to ignore his proximity during the long nights ahead. It wasn't going to make a difference where he slept, she thought with a rueful glance at the sofa bed. Whether he was on the bed beside her or on the couch or on the floor, she was sure she'd remain awake as long as they continued to share the bedroom.

Later that night, having lost the argument about who would sleep in the bed, Melina had ample proof she'd been right about the sofa bed. Every time Adam turned over trying to find a comfortable place, or stifled a long, drawn-out sigh, her body heated. It wouldn't have taken much persuasion on his part for her to ask him to join her—if her heart hadn't already been set on giving herself only in the act of love.

ADAM BREATHED A SIGH of relief when the following two weeks sped by without his breaking his promise to Melina. The more he thought about the promise, the more he realized the right thing to do was to let Melina choose which direction their relationship would take. Left to him, he would have shown her how much he had begun to care for her.

Melina, thank God, had gone ahead to establish a daily routine for the three of them. Jamie, though obviously not happy at not always having her own way, had managed to behave herself. Having Melina care for his daughter sure made life a lot easier. But he was a man as well as a father. His manhood ached for this lovely new woman in his life.

The only promising spot on the horizon was the telephone call he'd had this morning from his ex-wife. Back from her honeymoon, she'd asked if Jamie could come home for the weekend to meet her new half siblings. He hated to let Jamie go, but it *was* a chance for him and Melina to get accustomed to each other.

"The choice to spend the rest of the summer with me is open, sweetheart," Adam announced after he'd explained that the man Jeanette had married had come with two young daughters and a nine-to-five job. "I'd like you to stay for the rest of the summer, but it's up to you."

Jamie shot out of her chair, a big smile on her

piquant face. "I'll come back to visit, Daddy, I promise. It's just that I don't have anyone to play with here like I will have at home."

"Come." Melina held out her hand as she exchanged smiles with Adam at the way Jamie had suddenly come alive. "I will help you pack your things."

As an only child for the first five years of her life, Melina had to sympathize with Adam's daughter. The birth of her own two brothers had not only given her live dolls to play with, it had taken some of the heat off of trying to be daddy's good little girl. This was Jamie's chance to be part of a large family.

"I'll take Jamie home to her mother," Adam told her. "I have to stop by my company warehouse for a few minutes. When I come back, I'll show you some parts of San Francisco I've always enjoyed."

Melina perked up. Sight-seeing was fine, but the idea of seeing a part of Adam's life would help her understand him. Perhaps, even give them a chance to get to know each other better. "Perhaps you could pick me up first so I could go with you to the warehouse, no?"

"Sure." Adam smiled at the enthusiasm on Melina's face. His new wife seemed more excited at the opportunity to learn about his interests than his exwife had ever been. Claiming she couldn't take the strong scents of the imported products, Jeanette had visited the warehouse only once.

Jamie, carrying her little suitcase in one hand and holding her father's in the other, hesitated when it came time to say goodbye to Melina. "Can I take some of the cookies I made home with me?"

"Of course." Melina led the way to the kitchen and packed a small plastic container with the Greek butter cookies. "There, now they will stay nice and fresh."

"How about a thank-you to Melina for teaching you how to bake the cookies?" Adam regarded his daughter with a raised eyebrow. "Better yet, how about a goodbye kiss?"

"Thank you for the baking lessons, and for the cookies, Melina," Jamie said dutifully. "Can we bake some more when I come back?"

"Of course. I have many recipes I would like to teach you." Melina smiled. A little girl was a little girl the world over.

Apparently won over, at least for now, Jamie raised her cheek for an air kiss. "Will you be here when I come back?"

Melina's eyes locked with Adam's enigmatic gaze. His lack of expression reminded her of their bargain. She might be here when Jamie returned, but she was to remain only until she obtained her green card. Any hint of affection she'd sensed from Adam before was gone. Or, it was a signal that the nature of their relationship would be up to her.

*"Yeiasou pedaki mou,"* she told Jamie with a tender smile before she went on to translate. "In my language, I am saying 'goodbye to you, my little child.' I hope we will meet again soon." She fingered a lock of Jamie's flyaway hair from her brow and kissed her there.

At the scene taking place in front of him, Adam's heart thundered in his chest. There was no way he could describe the rush of feeling that ran through him at Melina's tender goodbye to his little girl. This was what he'd hoped for. This was what he'd allowed himself to miss.

THE LARGE Adam Blake International Foods warehouse was built at the edge of San Francisco Bay. Just south of the ferry wharf, it appeared to be in the center of the city's international import/export business. To Melina's pleased surprise, the busy area looked like Piraeus, Athens's port city.

She hung back to gaze around her and recalled the days when she was a little girl and had accompanied her father to Piraeus when he'd arranged for shipping the pistachios from the Kostos family orchard. She'd dreamed of traveling to faraway places even then, with no real chance of the dream coming true. Until she'd overheard Adam in the embassy elevator.

She noticed Adam watching her. "This reminds me of my childhood." She went on to describe her visits to Piraeus with her father.

"Gets into your blood, doesn't it?" Adam smiled and took her hand. "Once I came down here and saw that this was an exciting little world all its own, I was hooked. The activity, the sounds and the scents of products from around the world got to me. It's still there."

Melina looked at him sympathetically. "My father is a man like you," she said. "But I think the only reason he stays home instead of traveling on business is because of my mother. Even now that my brothers and I are grown."

"Maybe I should have followed your father's example," Adam replied ruefully. "But then," he said as a smile curved his mouth, "we wouldn't have met."

Melina blushed and her heart skipped a beat or two. Until now, rather than falling head over heels with Adam, her heart had been taking tiny steps. Now, it took a giant step. She nodded and smiled.

"Shall we go on?"

"Of course," Melina said, happy that Adam had forgotten to let go of her hand.

There were signs in English and various Asian

languages on the many buildings of the import/export companies that lined the street. The huge sign on Adam's building was in both English and Greek.

The streets were crowded with shouting stevedores and streams of delivery trucks fighting for space. The lingering scent of newly caught fish and fresh spices hung in the air.

Above the din, the noise of competing foreign languages reminded her of how much she missed her native land.

She inhaled a deep breath of the salty air. "I didn't realize how much I missed my country until now."

"Wait until you're inside my warehouse," Adam promised. "It's about as close to Greece as you can come and still be here in San Francisco." He opened a door and led her inside.

The warehouse was a two-storied, climate-controlled building with wooden flooring that had absorbed the spicy scents of the imported commodities that had been stored inside over the years.

The main floor, with Adam's office in one corner, was divided into sections. One section was marked Wine. On closer inspection, Melina noted each bottle of wine from Greece carried a label showing the year the grapes were harvested. Some carried the name of her native village of Nafplion.

Condiments and nuts filled another marked-off

section. To Melina's pleasure, there were several canvas sacks of pistachios imprinted with her family's name, Kostos. Spices and olive casks occupied other spaces. Fresh cheese, in casks of brine were in still another area. The largest section was devoted to the virgin olive oil for which her country was so famous. The scent of finely ground coffee also hung in the air.

She inhaled a deep breath and, noticing Adam's interested gaze, smiled her appreciation. "If I close my eyes, I could believe I was back in my father's warehouse in Nafplion."

"I'm glad," he said, pleased to have put a smile on Melina's face. "I've had a few misgivings about taking you away from familiar surroundings. But," he added playfully, "it looks as if it's a small world, after all."

Absorbed in investigating her surroundings, Melina nodded. In one corner, a group of statuary depicted Greek mythological heroes, with and without concealing fig leaves. She blushed at statues of entwined lovers.

"Interesting, aren't they?" Adam said wryly. "Actually, outside of Greek virgin olive oil, these statues are among my best sellers."

"I don't doubt it," Melina replied as she eyed one particular amorous plaster couple. "Their expressions are so real, they actually seem to be in love.''

Adam joined her in gazing at the foot-high statue of two people, their bodies embracing, gazing into each other's eyes. For his money, he thought as his own body warmed, Melina was right on target. The artist had captured a yearning expression on the faces.

The feelings depicted were so real, Adam found himself turning to gaze at Melina. He'd never claimed to be an expert on the subject of love, but after seeing the emotions filtering across her face and sensing her thoughts, he was beginning to think there might already be something more to their relationship than convenience.

Any hope of keeping the way he felt about Melina in check vanished. Judging from the rapt expression on Melina's face, maybe *this* was the right time to show her instead of telling her how much he was attracted to her. Best of all, he thought with a close look at Melina's interest in her surroundings, the statues provided the perfect stimulus for seduction.

Melina turned from the statue as Adam's arms encircled her. Her lips parted and her eyes opened wide. Slowly, oh so slowly, her gaze met his. He wanted to kiss her into rapture as her head nestled at his throat and he inhaled the scent of love, her scent and the scent of the Greece he loved.

He knew it was wrong to want Melina with every breath he took, but she was made to be loved. He had to hold her in his arms, to show her how much he'd grown to care for her. But love?

After his first unhappy venture into marriage, he wasn't sure he could give the love she deserved. What he should feel for her, he told himself, was gratitude for her caring nature. Instead what he felt was a desire that was setting him on fire.

He took her by the hand, pulled her against the full length of his body.

"Adam?"

The hesitancy in her voice told him she sensed what he was thinking. He sensed that Melina longed to give in to the fire he saw reflected in her eyes.

"The other day you said we were strangers?" She nodded slowly, her eyes wide, a blush covering her cheeks. "That might have been true three weeks ago, sweetheart, but we have been living together ever since then. So, I think this is a good time for us to really get to know each other. Of course," he added as he held her closer and smiled down into her luminous eyes, "you can always say no."

"No. I mean, yes," She smiled up at him and raised her lips for his kiss. "Maybe this *is* the time and the place to get to know you better," she teased. "After all, you are my husband, Adam *mou.* I desire you for my lover, my only lover."

With a murmured word of reassurance, Adam

lowered his lips to hers. He lightly brushed her lips with his and kissed her, then deepened the kiss.

She put her arms around his neck and kissed him back with all the joy she felt in her heart. She heard a growl of pleasure from the back of his throat.

"I want you, Melina," he said. "No pretense, no promises about tomorrow. Let's think only of now, today," he murmured as he ran his hands across the nape of her neck, wrapping her hair around his hand.

Melina sighed when his tongue swept her lips as he bent to kiss the valley between her breasts. Promises? As far as she was concerned, he'd already made them back in Athens.

"I love you," she answered softly, even though she sensed he was too deep into passion to have heard her. Maybe Adam wasn't promising forever, but in her mind at least, these moments were her forever. This was the moment she'd dreamed of since she became a woman. And Adam was the man with whom she'd dreamed of someday sharing the moment.

A haze of pleasure ran over her as Adam picked her up and carried her to his office and to the leather couch. "You're sure about this?" he asked with a tender smile. "You still have a chance to say no."

"I'm sure," she said, her lavender eyes glowing.

Adam saw her trembling fingers hesitate at her lips. Asking her to undress wasn't an option. "Here, let me," he said softly. He lifted her blouse over her head and kissed her bare shoulders. "All right?" She nodded shyly. He put his arms around her, unbuttoned her bra and slowly dragged the straps from her body. "Beautiful," he murmured as he caressed her bare shoulders. "Do you want me to stop?"

Stop? Melina shook her head. Not when she'd mentally rehearsed this moment ever since she'd realized that she'd fallen in love with Adam. And once she'd dare to dream that her marriage of convenience might become a real one. All her questions, all her reservations, abruptly vanished with the sensuous sound of Adams's voice murmuring affectionate words in her ear.

Never taking his eyes from her, Adam tore off his clothes and dropped them to the floor. As if on second thought, he picked up his shirt and draped it across the leather couch in an open invitation for her to join him there.

Melina's heart pounded. Would Adam think her beautiful? Would he still want her when he found she'd never been with another man?

Rational thought vanished as Adam enfolded her in his arms and kissed the corners of her eyes. He ran his hands over her shoulders, waist and hips. He cupped her bottom and pulled her closer until she could feel his hard arousal. Melina shuddered with desire.

"I can't get enough of you," Adam murmured as he bent to kiss her breasts then lifted his lips to hers.

He then lowered her to the shirt-covered couch and followed her down.

He cradled her in his arms, kissed her chin, the nape of her neck and the hollow between her breasts. The strength of his arms, his hard, ready body against hers, took her down a path she'd never known before.

The male scent of him, the sound of his low, sensuous voice whispering love words into her throat sent coherent thought tumbling out of her mind. This couldn't be wrong. She couldn't help herself. She'd never made love before, but some innate instinct urged her to caress him. To show him with all her heart that she was ready to be his wife.

With a groan of pleasure, Adam nudged her legs apart and rewarded her with a slow and lethal smile that lit up the dim room. "Are you okay with this?" he asked tenderly as he caressed the inside of her thighs and stroked the sweet, wet center of her. "I can't get enough of you, sweetheart," he repeated.

Breathless with desire, Melina nodded. Every nerve in her body cried out for the pleasure that she knew only the man who was her husband could give her.

When Adam made her his, Marina's last coherent thought was that she wasn't going to have enough of him, either.

## Chapter Eight

Lost in a golden haze of happiness, Melina finally roused herself from where she lay with her head on Adam's chest. She studied the man who had become so dear to her in so short a time. She'd always been a romantic person, but now Adam's lovemaking had released some unknown depth of emotion within her.

Smiling, she silently thanked the Fates that had put her at his side at the right moment. The moment when she'd heard Adam remark to Peter Stakis that he intended to find someone to care for his daughter Jamie. She silently thanked Peter for suggesting Adam get married instead of hiring a housekeeper or a nanny.

She gently stroked Adam's still heated skin, saying, *"S'agapo, agapee mou."* When Adam didn't seem to understand, she repeated, "I love you, my love.'' Instead of the soft look of love she expected to see on his face, he remained deep in thought.

"Adam?'' Her questioning gaze rested on Adam as he pulled away from her. Cold chills ran down her spine. Whatever he was thinking, it wasn't about love.

"We need to talk.'' Clearly puzzled, he gazed down at her. "Why didn't you tell me this was your first time?''

Melina's heart sank, the warm feeling lingering in her middle fading. Instead of being pleased that he had been the first man to love her, he sounded as if she'd deliberately misled him. Bewildered at the sudden change in him, she pulled back. "What difference would it have made? We are man and wife.''

Adam rubbed his brow. The difference was that he should have known from the very beginning of their unusual relationship that Melina had been a virgin. He should have recalled how sweet and naive she'd been the first time they'd kissed. An innocent like Melina wouldn't know how the nostalgic setting and the erotic statuary, intended as mere tourist pieces, could lead to his making love to her.

More to the point, he damned himself for fulfilling her father's accusation that Adam had compromised his daughter. What kind of man did that make him?

Damn! He should have realized that with Melina's old-country upbringing, she would have interpreted his making love to her as an intention to turn their marriage of convenience into a real and lasting union.

Unfortunately, no matter how strongly he was drawn to her, anything permanent was out. Besides, she'd already indicated that her goal in marrying him was only to obtain a green card, hadn't she?

How could he have been so stupid to have set himself up for another failure?

"It's not your fault, Melina, it's mine," he finally said, hating himself for the wounded look that replaced the glow of happiness in her eyes. "I knew better. I shouldn't have touched you. I should have kept my promise."

"You did not enjoy making me your true wife?" Melina regarded him with a crushed look, enough to make a man hate himself. "I thought most men wanted a pure woman for a wife and for the mother of their children. Is it not the same here as it is back in Greece?"

Children! Adam's heart sank even further. He hadn't stopped to think of the future. "Yes, of course," he said, "but that's not the point. We made a bargain, I should have kept it."

He didn't have an excuse for making love to Melina. The truth was it looked as if he had begun to fall for Melina. Another no-no.

He could have blamed the suggestive statuary for the impulse to take Melina in his arms. Or even the passion that had glowed in her eyes as she'd gazed at the figures and then at him. But the figures were made of plaster, frozen in time. He was flesh and blood. He should never have allowed himself to get so carried away.

"That's not the point," he finally said. He didn't have an excuse for making love to Melina. The truth was he'd wanted to. Another no-no if he were an honorable man. "We made a bargain. I should have kept it."

"A bargain? The no-touching-in-private bargain?" She looked incredulous. "You are kidding, no?"

She was right to doubt him, Adam thought ruefully. What man in his right mind would have remembered their bargain at a time like this?

Adam winced. "As ridiculous as it seems now, yes." In hindsight, he should have known that committing to such an unrealistic bargain with such an appealing woman as Melina would have eventually become impossible. Her Greek background, her lilting, soft accent and her foreign manner had drawn him like a magnet almost from the first time he'd met her.

Melina was a lovely woman who personified everything a man could ask for in a mate. But he had felt the same way about Jamie's mother…in the beginning. Was he willing to risk his heart again?

"That bargain was made before you decided to make me your true wife," Melina said in a sweet voice that made his senses spin out of control all over again. "Surely it does not apply now." She was right. He felt more like a heel than ever.

The genuine hurt that had replaced the passion in Melina's expressive lavender eyes hit Adam in the middle of his gut. She actually thought he didn't care for her! The truth was something else. How could he explain, now that he'd taken them beyond the point of no return, that the prospect of eventually losing her after she obtained the green card should have been ample reason for his not making love to her?

He had no way of knowing if she really meant it when she said she wanted to be his true wife, anyway. She may have made heart-stopping love with him, but she'd never actually said she intended to remain his wife after she got what she truly wanted.

Adam briefly considered the hopeless situation. He was a man, after all. Only a man without blood in his veins could have ignored the fire that burned within Melina.

To add to his chagrin, now that they'd consummated their marriage, a quiet annulment was out of the question. How could he have allowed his traitorous body to rule his mind? He'd let his emotions dominate him and he was going to have to face the consequences.

Another divorce loomed on the horizon.

His earlier divorce from Jeanette had left a scar he'd sworn never to repeat, for Jamie's sake and his own.

It wasn't as if he hadn't tried to keep the marriage to Jamie's mother together, he had. He'd concentrated on working long and difficult hours to provide the life he'd thought she'd wanted. Instead, it had turned out that what his ex-wife had wanted had been him. All he'd gotten for his hard work had been the divorce and the dubious distinction of becoming a part-time father. He'd gotten used to the idea of living alone—until Melina had come into his life and shown him what he'd missed.

Now what?

Bottom line, he had to keep his distance from Melina from now on. If it wasn't already too late.

He forced himself to slide off the couch and to dress. Once he had made his peace with Melina, he would do whatever it took to keep their ultimate and inevitable parting friendly. "I'm afraid it's time to go."

Watching warring emotions cross Adam's face as

he dressed, made Melina's heart shatter into a million little pieces. Before she'd made love with him, she'd made a silent commitment to be his wife in all ways. Tonight she had given him her heart and her soul—how could he have rejected her?

Now that he'd made her a true wife, she couldn't let their meeting end like this. "Don't go, Adam. You are right. We need to talk. Can we not remain here a little bit longer?"

"No, I'm afraid not." Adam made a show of glancing at his watch. "The night watchman will be making his rounds soon. If he sees a light in here at this hour, he'll think something is wrong."

Adam's voice sounded remote and as cold as the band of ice that had formed around her heart, Melina thought sadly as she groped for her clothing. How could their encounter have begun so magically yet ended so badly? Where was the man who had shown her the paradise possible between a man and a woman?

THE NEXT MORNING Adam begged off from the breakfast Melina had prepared for him. "Sorry, I have to go to work. I'm late for a meeting at the warehouse with some new buyers."

"At least coffee?" Melina waited while Adam hurriedly gulped down a cup of hot, black coffee. "When will you be home?"

"I'll probably be gone all day." Adam avoided her eyes as he picked up his briefcase and headed for the door. "If you do go out, don't wander too far. You wouldn't want to get lost."

Tears formed in Melina's eyes as the door closed behind Adam. If he only knew, she felt lost already.

She sensed that there was more to Adam's leaving for the entire day than a meeting with buyers. From the way he'd avoided her eyes when he said good-bye, she was afraid he wanted to put a distance between them. After their wonderful love tryst yesterday afternoon, how could he behave as if they were strangers?

Her only hope for the future lay in the fact that Adam, even with Jamie's bed available for a few days, had chosen to sleep on the sofa bed in their room. For appearances' sake, just in case they had unexpected visitors, he'd muttered before he'd said good-night.

With Adam gone and without the lively presence of Jamie, the town house became an empty shell, not the home she'd dreamed of making for him. She wandered through the house and studied the pristine kitchen, the picture-perfect rooms and the empty child's bedroom. There was no reason to remain inside, she thought as she found the telephone book and looked up an address. Surely the answer to her dilemma could be found there.

Her heart lightened when the location map in the phone book showed the Greek Annunciation Cathedral on Valencia Street near the Papadakis Greek Grocery Store. She'd been to the store with Adam. Surely she could find her way there again.

THE DOORS to the cathedral, with its vaulted ceilings and beautiful windows, stood open. Inside, the shadowed interior was lit with shafts of multicolored sunlight streaming in through the stained-glass windows. The scent of burning candles filled the air. A few people, scattered throughout the church, were deep in prayer. An attendant was placing fresh flowers at the altar.

Melina found a pew at the back and sat to think. She had to find a way to make Adam understand what they had together was too precious to toss away over a misguided bargain. A bargain she'd discovered she no longer wanted.

Moments went by. Until Melina realized she wasn't going to get an answer for her heartbreak. The answer had to come from using her common sense. The strength and wisdom to make her marriage succeed had to come from within her, her rational mind told her, not from the church's scented air. With love and patience, she had to persuade her husband to forget a foolish bargain made before they'd gotten to know each other.

The answer became suddenly simple. The problem between them had to have been brought about by the differences in their language and their cultural backgrounds. And their lack of candor. They had to talk. But when? And how?

She recalled her mother's down-to-earth advice about staying happily married and the way to a man's heart. "Feed him well and he will be yours forever," her mother always said.

Newly optimistic, Melina slipped out of the cathedral and hurried to the Papadakis store. She would make Adam a special dinner to soften him up before they talked. If her mother's advice worked as well with Adam as it had seemed to work with her father, Adam would beg her to stay with him as his true wife.

Josef Papadakis greeted her like a long-lost relative. "Ah, Madame Blake! Good afternoon!" He bowed her into the store and shouted for his wife. "Katherine, come and see who has come to visit us! It is good to see you again!" he told Melina with a broad smile.

Melina's spirits rose at the greeting and her down-home-like surroundings. The store, the familiar scent of spices and the welcome smile on Mrs. Papadakis's face made her feel at home. Before she knew it, Melina found herself explaining her mission. "So you see, I wish to make a special dish of *pastitso* for my husband. He loves Greek food. It must be the best Greek dinner he has ever had.''

Papadakis nodded wisely. "You are a good *yenaika*," he said. "Your husband is a lucky man to have found a good Greek wife like you."

With a conspiratorial smile, his wife led Melina to the refrigerated counter. Enthusiastically, her husband strode through the store placing small elbow macaroni, tomato paste, allspice, nutmeg and cinnamon in a shopping bag.

Katherine handed Melina the wrapped package of ground beef. "You have butter, lemon, eggs and milk to make the sauce, yes?"

Melina thought for a moment. She'd already bought some of the ingredients to make cookies. "A fresh lemon?"

"Ah." Katherine hurried to a fresh fruit and vegetable display. "Fresh lemon juice is best…it brings out the taste of the sauce. Anything else?"

Melina shook her head. She could hardly wait to get back to the town house to start making the Greek version of lasagna.

"No Greek dinner is complete without some of my appetizers," Josef said firmly. "And some Greek wine to soften up your husband." Papadakis winked.

Katherine burst into a flow of comments to her husband in Greek.

Papadakis grinned.

Melina blushed.

"You will need to whet your husband's appetite for you." An unrepentant Papadakis led the way to jars of caviar, marinated artichoke hearts and Greek olives. Over Melina's objections, he added them to the shopping bag. "Now," he announced as he added a can of anchovies with a flourish, "you have everything you need to bring your husband to his knees. The rest is up to you." He burst into laughter when his wife swatted him on his shoulder.

"*Efcharisto!*" Red-faced, Melina thanked the pair and backed out of the store before Josef Papadakis could give her more intimate advice. Was it only Greeks who were not ashamed to speak of love and lovers as if they were an everyday topic of conversation?

An hour later, with the *pastitso* finally in the oven, the table set for two, the wine in its cooler and the overhead lights appropriately dimmed, Melina started for her room to dress for the special occasion. One way or another, Adam was in for the surprise of his life.

The doorbell rang. Half dressed, with only a filmy robe over her brief bra and matching bikinis, Melina peeped through the security hole.

A man dressed in a navy-blue-striped business

suit and woman in a tailored dress stood there, briefcases in hand. "Mrs. Blake?"

Melina reluctantly opened the door. Before she could speak, the man held out a business card. "Thomas Webber, from the Immigration and Naturalization Service. The INS," he went on to explain. "And this is Ms. Camden."

Melina held her robe together with one hand and reached for the card. "I'm sorry, but my husband isn't at home," she said uneasily. Who would have thought the INS would have come visiting her at home? "I'm afraid he didn't tell me you made an appointment with him."

"As a matter of fact, we didn't, Mrs. Blake," Webber said, his eyes on the neckline of the robe. "May we come in?"

"Of course." Melina held open the door. Was something wrong? Her heart thudded in her chest.

Webber motioned his companion into the room and sniffed appreciatively. His eyes roamed the living room and finally settled on the small dining room table. Wine was cooling alongside the table and mauve candles waited to be lit.

"Special occasion?" he asked, his eyes back to skimming her informal attire.

Melina blushed and pulled the neck of her robe more tightly.

"Knock it off, Tom," Ms. Camden said in an

undertone, though loud enough for Melina to hear. "Mrs. Blake is a newlywed, after all."

"That's precisely what we're here to verify," Webber answered stiffly. "And why," he added with a stern glance at his companion, "we usually try to visit unannounced. Caught unaware, people tend to tell the truth."

"I have nothing to hide," Melina said. Webber raised an eyebrow. Melina blushed as she realized her double entendre. She gathered her sheer robe more tightly around her.

Her pleasure in creating a special night for herself and Adam rapidly dimmed. Instead of sharing the perfect night with Adam, there would now be the intrusion of the INS to contend with. "Please sit down. If you'll excuse me, I'll go and dress. I'll be back in a moment."

Melina sighed as she glanced at the outfit lying on the bed. She'd intended to wear the sheer, seductive outfit tonight to attract and keep Adam's attention. No way was she going to put it on now and expose herself to Webber. She quickly dressed in a flowing skirt and a peasant-style blouse, ran a comb through her hair and returned to the living room.

Ms. Camden sniffed and motioned to the kitchen. "Something burning?"

Melina rushed to take the blackened *pastisto* out of the oven. Grim, she set the pan in the sink and covered it with a clean dishtowel. So much for having a romantic dinner with Adam. She shook her head and went back to her inquisitors.

"Let's start at the beginning." Webber opened his briefcase, took out a folder and studied it for a long, intimidating moment. "You and Mr. Blake have been married for roughly a month?"

Melina's heart sank as she folded her hands in her lap and nodded.

"Do you mind telling me where and how you and Blake met? How long had you known each other before the marriage?"

Melina listened to the barrage of questions and silently prayed for Adam to come home soon. The loaded questions were coming faster than she could think, let alone answer. What really began to bother her was that not once did Webber refer to Adam as her husband.

"Surely, that is all on record," she said, indicating the folder. "I am sure I answered all the questions when I filled out the application for the green card."

Webber smiled politely and raised an eyebrow. "Tell me again." His pen was poised above the folder.

Melina closed her eyes and tried to focus on an answer. She and Adam had been so caught up in trying to make Jamie happy that they hadn't had a chance to decide on a story that would pass muster should anyone ask. For that matter, she hadn't thought anyone would care. Adam was an American citizen and well-known businessman. Who would suspect him of concocting a mock marriage? What about their marriage had drawn the attention of the INS? Melina wondered. No one but Adam and herself, with perhaps Peter Stakis, knew the truth. Peter would never have informed on her, he was just as much a romantic as she was.

"I worked at the United States embassy for two years," she replied. "My husband regularly came through the embassy on business. We met there."

"Our investigation showed your position at the embassy was in the process of being downsized when you announced you were leaving."

"I was to be married, and my husband had to return home."

"You never considered marrying Blake prior to that day?"

"I accepted my husband's marriage proposal at the time he made it," she said, determined to remind Webber that she and Adam were husband and wife.

"In time for a one-day honeymoon in Corfu." Webber read from the folder. "Are you sure the marriage isn't a sham? An agreement that, as the wife of an American citizen, could get you a green card?" When she didn't answer, he went on. "You do know, don't you, that it can take two years before a green card is issued?''

At the mention of the honeymoon fiasco and the length of time she and Adam would have to live together, Melina almost lost her cool. The marriage, the honeymoon and her stay with Adam in San Francisco had left a series of questions in her mind. So, why not the INS? Still, she thought as her frosty gaze locked with Webber's, the events were no one's business but her own. And Adam's.

All the more reason for her to have a soul-searching talk with Adam as soon as possible. She had to clear up any misunderstandings between them, and the only way to do that was to make him listen to her.

She was going to tell him so in no uncertain terms as soon as she laid eyes on him.

To Melina's relief, Ms. Camden finally broke in. ''I don't know, Tom. This looks like a real love affair to me,'' she said enviously, gesturing to the table set for a romantic dinner. ''It doesn't come any better than that.''

Webber sniffed. ''On the surface, maybe. Now, back to the subject. As far as I'm concerned, there seems to be something phony about your rush into marriage, Mrs. Blake. We've had a number of foreign nationals brought to this country under one pretense or another. Are you sure you weren't coerced into coming here?''

To Melina's relief, and just in time, she heard a key turn in the door. Adam was home! She jumped to her feet and rushed to meet him. She had to find a way to warn him Webber had done his homework and appeared suspicious of the way she and Adam had met and married! She had to somehow tell Adam the story she'd told Webber. She had to make sure Adam's story matched hers. If it didn't, she would be deported back to Greece before she had a chance to make Adam understand how much he'd come to mean to her!

# Chapter Nine

Banking on what Adam might have learned of the Greek language during his visits to Greece, Melina greeted him at the door. "Why are you so late?" She kissed him on his cheek. After the way they'd parted last night, he looked surprised. She didn't blame him, but she was desperate. Before he could say anything to give them away, she whispered in his ear, "*Prosehee,* be careful." She went on in her native language, "These people are from the immigration department."

To her relief, Adam put his arms around her. She didn't know how much he understood of what she was saying, but she continued. "They want to know how we met and why we married just when you were about to leave my country." She didn't have time to fill in any details, but she had to communicate the danger without giving herself away.

She pulled Adam into the living room where her

visitors had come to their feet. She laughed self-consciously. "Please excuse me. I am afraid I revert to my native language when I am exited. I was just explaining to my husband that you are from the immigration authorities."

Adam knew enough of what Melina had whispered to understand that she was deeply upset by their visitors. It wasn't until she said "immigration authorities" that his antenna really began to quiver.

Judging from the apprehension on Melina's face, Adam sensed that she was afraid the INS didn't believe their wedding was legitimate. She was afraid she wouldn't qualify for that damned green card! Any hope that she might have changed her mind about leaving him after she got the card faded. It was clear Melina wanted that card more than she wanted him.

In spite of his reluctance about ending their unusual relationship, he still felt duty bound to help her. He'd not only taken her from her home to a foreign culture, he'd taken advantage of her vulnerability by making love to her. Now, he figured he owed her big. She had no one here in the United States to look out for her but him.

He put his arm around Melina and, for his visitors' benefit, laughingly chided her. "I'm afraid my wife doesn't realize I'm not as proficient in her language as she is in mine. Do you mind introducing yourselves?''

Webber appeared unmoved, but he held out another business card. ''Tom Webber, INS. My partner is Ms. Camden. We're here to investigate your getting married and bringing your wife here. The speed with which she's applied for a green card is unusual,'' he said after a meaningful glance at Melina.

''Ah-hh,'' Adam shrugged helplessly. ''I'm afraid I didn't get all that from what my wife was trying to tell me. What can I do for you?''

Webber hovered at the edge of his chair. ''Mind if we sit?''

Adam casually gestured to the chair. ''Sure. Melina, can you find some refreshments for our visitors?''

Melina hid her shaking hands in the folds of her skirt. ''Of course. I should have thought of that myself. Please forgive me.''

She left Adam to keep Webber busy and made for the kitchen. She had to get back quickly to make sure Adam gave the same answers to Webber's questions as she had. Lemonade and cookies, she muttered, distracted by the thought of what might be going on in the other room. She hurriedly lifted a pitcher of fresh lemonade out of the refrigerator and stopped to wipe a spill that ran down her skirt.

She added a few butter cookies to a plate and set the pitcher, cookies, glasses and napkins on a tray.

At the same time she silently prayed Adam had understood enough of what she'd told him in Greek, or, at least, would be able to follow her lead when the right time came.

Adam noted the strained smile on Melina's face when she returned. He took the tray out of her ice-cold hands and put it on the coffee table in front of Webber. He was sure that whatever Melina had told the INS people, it had been as close to the truth as she could have made it. But, heaven forbid, not the whole truth or they were both in trouble. He'd back her up…maybe with the added embellishment of a man supposed to be in love. If it came to a choice of feeding Webber's suspicions to nix the application or helping Melina, as he instinctively wanted to, Melina won, hands down. Even if it meant he would ultimately lose her.

He made small talk about the weather while Melina poured lemonade and passed around the plate of cookies. Once she was seated beside him on the couch, he eyed Webber. "Now, just what can I do for you?"

Webber wiped powdered sugar from the butter cookies off his lips with a napkin. He took a swallow of lemonade before he cleared his throat and looked down at his notes. "How long have you known Miss Kostos?"

"She's Mrs. Blake," Adam said with a tight smile. "We were married at the U.S. embassy about a month ago. I'm sure it's a matter of record by now. You can check, if you already haven't done so."

"Of course," Webber agreed. He made a note on the yellow legal pad on his lap. "Do you mind telling me how long you've known Mrs. Blake?"

Adam was stumped for an answer that wouldn't blow the application to hell. Until, out of the corner of his eye, he saw Melina raise her right hand and stroke her chin with two fingers. He tried not to look at her, but he couldn't help himself. Fascinated, he watched while she stopped to put a strand of her hair behind an ear and smoothe it into place.

Adam tried to put himself in Melina's mind. She had to be trying to tell him something, but what? Two fingers? Ears? He searched his own mind for the answer. What did two ears have to do with the question?

Melina's eyes narrowed as she patted her ear again.

The silence was broken when Webber cleared his throat and repeated his question.

"About two years," Adam said into Melina's relieved smile. "Give or take a week or two. Not intimately, of course." He grinned at Melina. "That part came after the wedding.'' He hated to embarrass her, but if that comment didn't convince Webber that he and Melina had known each other before the wedding and were true-blue happy newlyweds, nothing would.

Ms. Camden smiled. ''And you honeymooned on Corfu.'' She sighed into her lemonade. ''I understand it's the most beautiful of all the Greek islands.''

''That's why I chose the island for a honeymoon,'' Adam said. He eyed Melina with a knowing glance.

Melina blushed, but she kept the fixed smile on her face. He had to admire her.

''A marriage that came out of the blue and ended with a one-day honeymoon?'' Webber continued as he looked at his notes. ''Sounds precipitous, to say the least.''

Ms. Camden sighed again. ''How romantic.''

''Yes. I highly recommend Corfu for a honeymoon,'' Adam agreed. To make Ms. Camden's eyes really light up, he added, ''Although one day was hardly enough.''

This time, Ms. Camden blushed.

Adam was pleased at the effect of his theatrics, but looking back to Corfu, he wondered how he could have resisted Melina in such a setting. And how he could have left Corfu behind for San Francisco.

Webber shot his partner a stern look before he turned back to Adam. "And Mrs. Blake's family? Have you met them?"

Adam nodded. "Yes, the day before the wedding." Thank goodness Webber had no way of knowing that the meeting with Melina's father had gone poorly. Or that Adam had changed his mind about crying off the wedding to protect Melina's reputation.

"Our investigations show that the Kostos live in a small village and are a very traditional family. How did they take this sudden marriage to a foreigner?"

"It wasn't sudden at all." Adam winked at Melina. "I'd been thinking about asking Melina to marry me for a while, but with all the traveling I do in my business, I kept putting it off.

"Of course, when I found I had to return to the States in a matter of days, I decided to pop the question and take her with me. As for Melina's family, they were sorry to see her leave her native country, but in the end they seemed pleased enough."

Adam had felt Melina's hand tighten on his at Webber's question about her family. Fear and uncertainty had made her hand slippery. Heaven help them both if Webber decided to interview Melina's father.

Webber's eyes narrowed. "What was the sudden emergency that brought you home?"

"My ex-wife called and told me she was getting married. She asked me to come home and care for our daughter while she was gone on her honeymoon."

"Ah! You needed a nursemaid?"

"No," Adam said coolly. "I needed a wife."

Adam put his arm around Melina and hugged her for a long moment, then finally turned to Webber. "If that's all you need to know for now, why don't we take this interview downtown? Maybe in a couple of days?" He made a show of glancing at the small dining room table, the wine cooler full of melted ice and the unlit candles. "I'm sure you can understand my wife and I have a special occasion to celebrate?"

Webber looked up from his notes. "An occasion to celebrate?"

"Yes." Adam put his arm around Melina. "Our one-month anniversary, as you so aptly pointed out a few minutes ago."

Webber closed his portfolio and stood. "I won't beat around the bush, Mr. Blake. Your sudden marriage to a virtual stranger, and a foreign national at that, is unusual. That leaves me with a few suspicions.''

"Such as?"

"It's against the law to import foreign labor," Webber said succinctly.

Adam's inside froze as he realized his career, and maybe his freedom, were on the line. "I'd hardly call my marriage importing foreign labor," he said. "As my wife, the only labor involved will be taking care of me and, on every other weekend and in the summer, my young daughter."

Webber cleared his throat. "I'm afraid I'll need to speak to you again. I'll have my office contact you for an in-depth interview. In the meantime, I suggest you both make yourselves available."

"Of course," Adam said blandly. He was seething inside as he gazed at Webber, the consummate bureaucrat. If Melina hadn't needed Webber's positive report, he would have been tempted to have decked the man by now. Experience had taught Adam that the lower the person stood on the official ladder, the more he wielded the little authority he had. Webber was a prime example.

He waited until the door closed behind the two immigration officials before he turned to Melina. To his surprise, tears lurked in her eyes. "What's the matter? Did I give the wrong answers to Webber's questions?"

"No," she said, her lips trembling into a smile. "You gave all the right answers. But I still worried." She gazed up at him. "I guess I shouldn't have. You know the laws of your country better than I do."

Adam cleared his throat. He should have been thinking about Webber's veiled threat, instead he was fighting to ignore his stirring libido.

It wasn't all his fault. Melina had a smile that could tempt a saint and, at the moment, the last thing he felt was saintly. He had to keep his wits about him instead of being drawn to her tearful eyes, bittersweet smile. He'd already seen how badly she wanted the green card. So, why the tears? How much further did she intend to carry this charade?

"Just a lucky guess," he answered with a shrug to hide the way he really felt. "It took me a few minutes to figure it out, but I finally asked myself why else would you be holding your ears if you didn't mean years?"

Melina looked chagrined. "I looked foolish, yes?"

"Yes...I mean, no," Adam said. He wanted to tell her she looked adorable, but a fat lot of good that confession would do for him. The harder he fell for Melina, the harder it would be to dig himself out of the mess he'd created. Instead he gazed at the decorated table. "Tell me, is tonight really the one-month anniversary celebration, or was it just a lucky guess?''

"Well, yes and no," Melina replied, looking happy again. "I decided to make you a special Greek dinner tonight. I confess I wanted to have your full attention while we talked," she added shyly.

Adam's eyebrows rose. If Melina only knew. She didn't need to try to seduce him with home-cooked Greek meals, wine and candles. To create a setting obviously intended to be intimate and romantic. She already had one hundred percent of his attention. He bit back his sensuous thoughts.

Too bad he couldn't make Melina's dreams come true without setting himself up for another heartache.

"I've had all the talking I can take for one day," he said more brusquely than he intended. "Besides, I thought we'd already come to an agreement. No more talking, no more touching. For both our sakes."

"Is it not better to talk than to behave as if we are strangers?" Melina asked.

"Melina," he said frankly, even as his heart thudded against his ribs. "We were strangers when we met and we're strangers still. Why don't we leave it that way?"

He hardened his heart against the bewildered look

that came across Melina's face. He had to do it. A clean break, for both their sakes.

He loosened his tie, raked his fingers through his hair and gestured to the dining room table. "Don't bother with dinner tonight. I'm sorry you went to so much trouble, but I'm not hungry. I caught something to eat down in the warehouse district."

"Not even a glass of wine and some Greek appetizers?"

"No thanks. To tell you the truth, I've had a rough day. I'm beat. I think I'll just turn in for the night." He shrugged off his jacket, threw it over his shoulder and headed for the bedroom.

Melina's heart skipped a beat when Adam hesitated at their bedroom door and stood a moment as if debating whether or not to go in. To her dismay he shrugged, turned and disappeared into Jamie's room.

If this was an indication of how he felt about turning their "marriage" into a real one, the answer was clear. He might have made marvelous love to her, but the chance of a future together was obviously over before it began.

Wordlessly, Melina cleared the table. She put the wine back into the refrigerator, dumped the burned *pastisto* into the garbage disposal and tossed the candles into a trash can. She was through trying to make Adam listen to her, to let her explain how little the green card meant to her, or anything else that would take her from him.

She was tired of trying to tell him that she wanted to keep the marriage vows. To forget the green card and to go on from there to create a family like the one she had at home.

Melina squared her jaw and thought back to the lessons of her childhood. She'd learned from a good teacher, her mother, that Greek women, while outwardly docile, were noted for their strength and their ability to create a happy family. She was her mother's daughter. It was her turn now. If not a family with Adam, then a full life on her own.

If Adam could play the marriage-of-convenience game with its no-touching-in-private bargain without becoming emotionally involved, so could she.

If he could ignore the strong physical attraction that sizzled between them every time their eyes met, so could she.

If he could lose himself in his work during his waking hours to avoid becoming involved with her, so could she. Two could play at Adam's game.

She would find a place to work where her lack of a green card didn't matter. The trick would be to find a place where she could be useful. A place where her Greek background and bilingual skills would be of value. Somewhere the INS would never think to look for her.

Papadakis's grocery store!

KATHERINE PAPADAKIS greeted Melina with open arms. *"Yeiasou!"* Tell me, how did your romantic dinner with your charming husband turn out?"

"He wasn't interested. Not in having dinner with me, or anything else," Melina said in Greek to the woman's growing horror. Somehow, speaking in her native language made the confession easier and more private. "My plans to get my husband's attention turned out to be a waste of time."

"No!" Mrs. Papadakis's eyes opened wide before she nodded knowingly. "That is because while your husband is a fine man, he is still an American. Greek men, God bless them, think with their heart, soul and body. American men think with—" She shook her head. "If only he had been a Greek, he would have listened to his heart. Like my husband, he would have shown you...but that is *allee historia,* another story." She sighed.

"I thought Adam was different," Melina said sadly. "We may have met and married in the space of three short days, but I soon became aware I was falling in love with him. I wanted a chance to tell him so."

Katherine Papadakis clucked her sympathy. "A true Greek man would never have been able to resist you. He would have known love knows no special time or place. And certainly not after you served him Greek wine and my husband's appetizers. And the *pastitso?*"

"I'm afraid I managed to burn it."

"*Alee thia!*" Katherine Papadakis crossed herself as her eyes narrowed. "Before or after he said he wasn't interested?"

Melina shrugged. "Before, but it didn't matter. He said he'd already eaten before he came home."

"Definitely not a Greek," the storekeeper's wife muttered. "Now…with my…" She smiled wickedly. "I have been thinking. I have an idea that will make your Adam change his mind."

"*Kai ego.* So have I," Melina said firmly. "But not for what you are thinking. For now, my idea has nothing to do with seducing my husband."

The last thing she wanted to hear was how to try to seduce Adam. She intended to make a new life for herself. At least, she thought smiling in satisfaction, she wasn't a twenty-nine-year-old virgin anymore.

"I don't have a green card yet," she went on, "but I've decided to find a job to keep myself too busy to care if I am left alone. Since you and your husband are part of the Greek community, I thought you might know if there is anyone who could give me work for a little while."

Melina waited hopefully while Mrs. Papadakis regarded her. She could tell the woman was eager to tell her new ideas of how Melina could seduce her husband, but Melina was firm. From now on, her marriage was going to be a business deal. Just as Adam seemed to want.

"God has sent you to us," the Greek woman finally said, nodding in satisfaction. "My husband has been called back to Greece…his father is ill. I remain here to run the store by myself. If you are willing, I could use a little help around the store while he is away."

"Without a green card?"

"No problem," Katherine said airily. "With my help and my connections, I'm sure we can get you a temporary work permit." She paused for a moment. "You are sure your husband won't care?"

Melina could hear her mother's independent, feisty spirit urging her on. Now was a good time to put the lessons to use that she'd learned at her mother's knee. No man ruled her mother. No man was going to rule her. The job offer was not only a golden opportunity to learn how to get around San Francisco, it would be good training for her future without Adam. A lonely future she'd foolishly bargained for.

She nodded proudly. "It doesn't matter. In this country, women seem to be free to choose how they spend their time. In any case, my husband will be too busy to even notice I'm gone during the day.''

"Then come, I will show you around the store." Katherine clucked sympathetically as she led Melina to the back of the store and handed her a pristine-white apron. "Here, put this on. You will look more like a grocery clerk." Satisfied with Melina's professional appearance, she went on. "Now, the good thing is that you speak Greek and are acquainted with everything in the store. The bad thing is, you are not acquainted with American money. Yes?"

Melina shook her head. "Not yet, but I intend to learn quickly. What else?"

Katherine smiled fondly. "You are a woman after my own heart," she said, patting Melina on the shoulder. "As long as you don't have your mother here, please allow me to think of you as my daughter. Please call me Katherine."

Melina hugged the solidly built woman. Katherine Papadakis reminded her of her own mother. Loving her would be easy. "It would make me proud, Katherine."

"Good. Now, the only thing to watch is that sometimes a customer is new to this country and will try to pay you in Euro dollars. The answer is no," she said firmly. "The value of the Euro changes too quickly. Send them to the bank and tell them to return for their purchases later."

The doorbell to the grocery jangled. Mrs. Papadakis urged Melina to the front of the store. "Go to work, my dear. For now, send the customer back here to me to pay."

Melina's mind whirled as she hurried to greet the customers lingering at the door. So much to learn, so little time to learn it. With her background and language skills, she knew she could easily handle the grocery clerk job. As for Adam, he would hardly miss her. The bigger problem facing her now was, could she handle only being Adam's phantom convenient wife without breaking her heart?

# Chapter Ten

Breakfast at seven with Melina. Polite talk.

Dinner at eight with Melina. More polite talk.

Adam stared moodily at the steaming soup bowl of meatball *avgolemono* and the plate of warm pita bread that Melina had set in front of him. For the past week she'd produced a series of Greek dishes he'd happened, at one time or another, to say he liked. He'd eaten his way through marinated chicken kebabs, roast leg of lamb with rice, a rich beef and potato moussaka and stuffed grape leaves. Last night, Friday, she'd served broiled fish with a lemon-herb sauce.

He loved everything Greek, but he'd reached the point where he would have given a week's salary to have a double-decker American cheeseburger and French fries smothered in ketchup. After she'd gone to such great lengths to please him, he just didn't have the heart to tell Melina so.

The silent treatment Melina was giving him was his fault for sure, but heaven help his digestive system. Enough was enough. He cleared his throat.

"How do you like our weather?" he asked casually. Weather had to be a safe topic.

"It is a little cooler than at my home in Greece," Melina said. "I think there is more rain here." She cocked her head and paused. "No?"

"No...I mean, yes," Adam replied, searching for another safe topic. When was he ever going to learn that "No?" meant she was asking if he agreed with her? What else did he have to learn about the woman who had rapidly taken over his heart and his mind?

"Are you enjoying San Francisco?"

"The little I've seen of it, yes," she said politely and returned to snagging a meatball out of her soup.

Adam felt guilty. He should have shown Melina something more of the city than the famous Fisherman's Wharf or the popular Pier 39. He should have taken the time to show her the true heart of the multinational city where people from all over the world had come to live. After all, unless she changed her mind, she was going to be living here for a while.

"I'm sorry," he said. "I'm sure I can find some time to show you some of my favorite haunts. San

Francisco is a city with many faces and I'd like to show them to you. That is, if you're up for it?''

"Someday when you are not so busy, perhaps." To Adams's pleasure, her eyes lit up. She went on to ask, "You have always lived in San Francisco?"

"Yes. Until I went into the import business and discovered the beauty of mainland Greece and the surrounding islands. I spend a great deal of my time there, both on business and pleasure." A perfect impersonal opening if there ever was one, Adam thought hopefully. "How about you?"

"I grew up in Nafplion and then lived in Athens. In my family, unmarried women do not usually leave home. I was an exception," she answered politely, but her eyes didn't meet his.

He felt disconcerted—and, worse yet, more guilty than ever for the sorry state of affairs between them. Even a discussion of the beauty of Greece or their childhood, didn't seem to really move her.

He tried again to break the silence that hung like a heavy curtain between them. "I'm looking forward to having Jamie back. How about you?"

"Of course. She is a lovely child."

He was running out of safe topics. He waited for her to pick up the conversation, but she continued to play with her soup.

Damn!

He recalled saying he didn't care to discuss their

sexual encounter, but he'd never expected the silent treatment and resulting frosty atmosphere between them. Not from a woman as full of fire as Melina. Even a verbal argument would be better than this.

He was desperate for a decent conversation, a hint that she was actually as aware of him as he was of her. Even a friendly word or two would help. What he wasn't looking forward to was being made to feel guilty for having made love to her.

Conversation aside, he had a bigger problem. If Melina's courteous replies or the frosty silence wasn't getting to him, the exotic scent, reminiscent of Greece, that clung to her was doing a number on him. To add to his physical and mental distress, he was ready to swear it was the same scent that filled the air when he'd taken her to visit his warehouse a week ago. A visit that had ended in the most memorable lovemaking of his life and, in retrospect, an encounter that had shown him what a treasure he could have in the fiery and sensuous Melina.

If only he'd kept his mouth shut and at least listened to what she'd had to say before turning her off. Afraid he would be taking advantage of her vulnerability and would only wind up losing himself in loving her again and again, he'd let his misguided nobility get the better of him.

Maybe it was his recollection of the scene in his warehouse that was working on him, but her body-stirring scent was driving him up the wall even now. So was she. Her proximity had left him with seven edgy days and sleepless nights. His awareness that the reason for his sorry condition had been sleeping in the adjoining bedroom wasn't helping, either.

Under cover of reaching for a slice of lemon to squeeze into the soup, he sucked in a deep breath of Melina's unusual scent. It wasn't any sweet-scented perfume, that's for sure. She hadn't been back to his warehouse, either.

Where could the mind-altering scent have come from?

Why did it cling to her?

And how in the hell was he going to cope with the effect it *was* having on him?

And why wasn't he smart enough to remember that, one way or another, any further intimate involvement with Melina could only come back to haunt him? Let alone dredge up unhappy memories of his previous marriage.

That wasn't the last of it, either. Why wasn't he able to remember trouble had already come knocking on his door? If Webber followed through on his suspicions, Adam might even land in the slammer for violating immigration laws. It wasn't only for Melina's sake that he was worried, he had a daughter to consider.

Legal marriage or not, it looked as if the INS

might already be considering charging him with importing illegal labor. Although why, after meeting Melina, would Webber even think he'd married her only to get unpaid labor was beyond him.

Adam stirred uneasily.

"Something wrong with the soup? I did not put in enough lemon juice?" Melina asked worriedly. She tasted a spoonful of her own soup and rolled the liquid around the inside of her mouth. "It tastes all right to me."

Adam groaned inwardly at the sight of her dainty pink tongue licking the corners of her lips. A long, lingering kiss would take care of those errant drops of the soup. But how was he going to get from polite dinner conversation to an intimate kiss unless they came to some kind of truce?

"No," he finally answered. "The soup is fine. Excellent. Everything you do is perfection." That much was true. The soup was more than fine, but he wasn't. Definitely not after seeing the sensuous movement of Melina's pink tongue at the corner of her mouth. And not when he yearned to kiss those lips.

"Then perhaps something else is wrong?" she asked, starting to rise. "I can make you something else."

"No thanks, this is great," he said hastily and went back to the soup. He was damned if he knew how to tell her he'd been thinking of asking her to put dinner on hold while he kissed her. After he'd foolishly agreed to place a limit on their private relationship, he'd only wind up looking like the idiot he was.

Bottom line, he'd had enough of polite talk. He'd also had enough of their estrangement.

"Melina," he said hopefully. "I'm waiting. Is there anything you'd like to say to me?"

She looked unconcerned. "I don't think so. Why?"

He wanted to tell her that he wanted his life back. Back to the time when he, Melina and Jamie had been on the verge of becoming a family. To the time before he'd decided that, for Melina's sake, the right thing to do was to honor that damnable marriage bargain.

Maybe, but he wasn't kidding himself. What he really wanted was Melina back in his arms and in his bed.

He just wasn't sure that was what Melina wanted.

Maybe she had been right the other day in the warehouse. Maybe it was time to swallow his pride and to really discuss their marriage.

He pushed the half-empty bowl of soup away and leaned across the table. "Melina," he said when he got her attention. "I've decided you could be right. Maybe it is time for us to have a heart-to-heart."

"Heart-to-heart?" Melina said, touching her breast with her hand. "What is this heart-to-heart?"

She looked so innocent of guile, Adam felt ashamed of himself. After the sweet way she'd made love with him, how could he have thought she had used him only to get the green card she'd said she wanted? The truth was, she'd been knocking herself out to keep her side of their bargain, while he'd been behaving like an ass.

She couldn't be that good of an actress, anyway. Not when he remembered the stars in her eyes as she'd welcomed him into her arms.

Heaven help him, he was tempted to give in to his earlier impulse. To put his doubts behind him and round the table. To grab Melina in his arms and to explain exactly how he was beginning to feel about her, and in great detail. Only he wouldn't stop with a verbal explanation. He'd show her just how much he *was* aware of her. To show her that he cared for her with all the passion in him.

"A heart-to-heart is an honest, open discussion of how we feel about our unusual situation," he explained carefully. "And what we think about all the other things in our life."

"What other things?"

"The two of us. And where you think our relationship is going."

"Are you sure this is what you want?" Melina

raised an eyebrow. "You might not like what you hear."

"True. I may not like what you say, but I still want to hear it."

A chill ran down Adam's spine as he thought of his possible sins of omission. Maybe being frank wasn't such a good idea, after all. Still, if it got Melina to talk, really talk to him, it was fine with him. Anything was better than the current cold freeze. "You go first. But before you start, I have a question."

She put down her spoon and sipped from a glass of water. "Go ahead."

"That scent you're wearing. It's driving me crazy. I've been trying to figure out where it comes from. And how it could have gotten on you."

Melina dropped her spoon, wiped her lips with a linen napkin and sat back. "You don't like it?"

"I like it," he assured her, trying to keep his emotions in check. He'd save telling her how he really felt about her smile, her scent and her melodious voice when it was his turn to bare his soul. "I like it fine. That's not the problem. It's just that I can't figure out where the scent could possibly come from."

"From the Papadakis's grocery store. Katherine Papadakis invited me to work there while her husband is away in Greece,'' she said, her tone defiant. ''I decided I needed to keep busy.

''Work? In the Papadakis's grocery store?'' Adam leaned over the table and sniffed again. Sure enough, Melina was surrounded by the aroma of exotic spices. No wonder they kept reminding him of the afternoon in his own warehouse.

Any effort to reestablish an intimate relationship with Melina suddenly took a back seat. Something more important was going on here. If he'd really paid attention to Melina this past week he would have figured what it was by himself.

''Since when?'' he asked, his manhood challenged. ''And why? For the money? You can have all the money you want—all you had to do is ask me.''

''Since I am not doing the job of taking care of Jamie, the job you hired me for, I did not wish to ask for money,'' Melina said proudly. ''Besides, you are always busy. When you're at work and even when you're at home, you are never available for me to speak to you. Even when you are here, your mind is somewhere else, until tonight.''

''You didn't need to find a job,'' Adam said, mentally chiding himself for not thinking of an allowance for Melina. ''You're my wife. You're doing a fine job of taking care of me right here.'' He sat back and regarded his not-so-convenient wife.

"Is that why you've been so quiet lately? Is that why you've been giving me the cold treatment? You want to shut me out of your life?"

"It was you who shut me out of your life," Melina said softly, and he heard the hurt in her voice. "After you made love to me, I thought surely things were going to be different. That we would have a true marriage. I was wrong. You've made it very clear you do not wish to have anything more to do with me."

"Wrong," Adam protested. Frustrated, he raked a hand through his hair. "The truth is, I was afraid I had taken advantage of you. In spite of the way things seem to have turned out, I *am* attracted to you. I'm pretty sure you feel the same way about me. Right?"

Melina gazed at him as if she could see right through him. What had he said wrong?

"It doesn't matter," she finally said. "You've made yourself very clear, but two can play at this relationship game, Adam Blake." She was proud of her use of the English language. "And before you ask, even in Greece, we know this expression of yours."

Her voice was calm, but Adam knew by the look in her eyes that she was hurt. If she had anything else on her mind, it wasn't going to be a confession of love. His Greek lioness was spoiling for a fight.

Adam abandoned the idea of persuading Melina she belonged in his arms. He threw down his napkin and tried to find the right words to strengthen their tenuous relationship. The situation was worse than he'd thought. How could he have been so dense? Surely he should have known there was more depth to Melina than to have sold herself merely for the right to work in the States.

He eyed her sitting there so proudly, so silently, so vulnerable. So hurt. She might dislike him now, but she had to have at least liked him a little from day one or she wouldn't have gone along with his off-the-wall marriage proposal.

"No matter what you believe, this isn't a game, Melina," he said. He knew that only by baring his soul and putting the past behind him was he going to have a chance to break that damn bargain. To make Melina his wife. "I was just trying to control myself the other afternoon. I didn't want to take advantage of you. You had bargained for a green card and I wanted you to have it. Take it from me," he added with a shaky laugh, "it hasn't been easy to stay away from you."

Melina's gaze seemed to soften for a moment, but at least she didn't turn away. He took heart. Maybe there was a chance for them, after all.

"As much as I've wanted to," he went on, "I've been reluctant to repeat our encounter the other day in the warehouse. I was afraid I was taking advantage of you at a very vulnerable moment. I was also afraid you'd think I was trying to persuade you to give up the idea of working in the States and to stick with me. I may have been stupid, but I decided I had to see to it that you got what you bargained for—a green card. I know better now."

"Is that all you thought of me? That I, as a woman who had never known another man before, would make love with you merely to ensure I would get a green card?"

Melina looked so hurt that Adam's heart turned over. "I know. I should have known better. But realizing you'd been a virgin until that moment took me by surprise. You were so beautiful, so tempting, surrounded by those erotic statues, I was afraid I'd taken advantage of you."

"And now?"

"I would like another chance to show you how I really feel about you. That's why I wanted a heart-to-heart, darling. To have a chance to explain that I've changed in ways I can hardly understand myself. Bottom line, I would like to know exactly how you feel about me, our future together and if you think you can put up with living here in the States— with me."

"I do not need this heart-to-heart. I already know how I feel," she said with a catch in her voice. "But you made it very clear—we have only a bargain, no real marriage. I am only trying to honor my end of it.''

''Forget the damn bargain!'' Adam said vehemently. ''That was then, this is now. I want to know exactly what you expect now, Melina. Just a green card? Or do you want more?''

Melina closed her eyes. Her hesitation scared the hell out of Adam. Was it really so hard for her to choose him?

''I want more than a green card,'' she finally whispered. ''I know what I asked for when we first spoke in Athens, but that was before I got to know you.'' Her gaze, fighting tears, locked with his. ''Things have changed. You are a good man, afraid to be rejected by another woman. I am not that other woman, Adam.'' Her expression saddened. ''You should know that by now.''

Adam started to rise to his feet to go to her when there was a strong, impatient knock on the door. Damn! Just when Melina's eloquent lavender eyes were speaking for her! And just when he was ready to swear that the unspoken words hovering on her lips were what he wanted most to hear.

He was tempted to ignore the knock. Unless the building was on fire, or whoever was out there had a more important need than he did, he didn't intend to answer the door. He didn't intend to let anything get between Melina and himself. He had to show her how deeply he felt about her. He wanted a happy ending to their meeting. And before the day was over, he intended to convince Melina that she wanted it, too.

The knock came again. This time stronger than ever. Whoever was outside wanted in—badly.

## Chapter Eleven

Adam tossed his napkin onto the table, glanced helplessly at Melina and strode to the door. On the other side of the peephole, the handsome, masculine face sporting a mustache belonged to a stranger. Heaven help him, he thought with a sinking heart, the stranger had a familiar Kostos trademark: sparkling lavender-colored eyes.

Adam had a sinking feeling that any chance of a reconciliation with Melina would have to wait. He had no choice but to open the door. "Yes?"

Andreas Kostos smiled broadly and threw his arms around Adam. *"Gabros moo!"*

Brother-in-law? "Melina's brother?" Adam asked cautiously when he was able to breathe again.

"I am Andreas, the older one," the man said with a broad smile. "The other brother is Christos!"

Adam vaguely remembered Melina's mentioning her two younger brothers, but this was the first time he'd met one of them. He peered over Andreas's shoulder. "Don't tell me he's here, too?"

His brother-in-law laughed. "No. Maybe later."

"Later?" Adam had visions of a Kostos family invasion with Andreas as the advance member. Since he'd already primed himself to apologize to his wife before he took her to bed to demonstrate his version of a heart-to-heart, a Kostos family invasion was the last thing he wanted. Thank God, it wasn't the senior Kostos.

"Of course. We are all anxious to see Melina again." Andreas looked over Adam's shoulder. "Is my sister at home?"

"Andreas!" Melina squealed at the sound of her brother's voice and came running to embrace him. "What are you doing here? Are you alone? How long can you stay?"

Andreas laughed, dropped his arms from around Adam's shoulders and reached for Melina. "Marriage hasn't changed you, Melina. You are still the little sister I remember."

"Little sister!" Melina playfully punched her brother on his shoulder. "I am five years older than you. I deserve some respect!"

"Older, perhaps, but still the excited little girl," her brother replied with a broad grin. He held her away from him and eyed her waistline. "So tell me, how is the baby coming along?"

Melina lost her smile and took a step backward. "What baby?"

"Papa said you were expecting a baby. No?"

Adam groaned. The senior Kostos had shouted the unforgivable when Melina had brought Adam home, but Adam had never expected the man actually believed it. The last thing Adam wanted was for Melina to remember it. Worse yet, for Melina to remember that until the moment Kostos had made the accusation, Adam had intended to back out of the wedding before the ceremony.

And maybe, just maybe, he was discovering that he was beginning to think of Melina in more of a romantic light than as a business bargain.

It had just taken him a while to realize he was falling in love with the most intriguing woman he'd ever had the fortune to meet.

Now this! Just when he was about to find out exactly how Melina actually felt about him. To find out if there was a chance of turning their marriage of convenience into a real one!

Before Andreas could answer Melina, Adam motioned his brother-in-law to wait a minute.

With a cautious look outside, Adam closed the door behind Andreas. "You're just in time for supper. Melina," he said, "how about getting your brother some of your delicious soup?"

"Of course!" With happy tears in her eyes, Melina rushed to the kitchen. *"Ella!"* she called over her shoulder. "Come, while the soup is hot."

Adam held Andreas back. "Hold on, Andreas," he said in an undertone. "Your father is wrong. Melina isn't expecting a baby. In spite of what he thinks, that's not why we got married."

"No?"

"No. Take it from me," Adam said fervently, "if Melina was expecting, I'd be the first to know."

Andreas regarded him with surprise. "Then why the hurry? Why did you not wait for a proper Greek wedding? Our mother was brokenhearted when Papa said—"

Adam sighed. "Trust me. It's a long, involved story. You don't want to know."

Andreas looked bewildered, not that Adam was surprised at the guy's reaction. Events were happening so fast, even he was having a hard time keeping facts together.

"I don't understand! I would not have asked if I did not want to know."

"Later," Adam murmured. "Come on in, before your sister thinks something is wrong."

Adam heard the sounds of Melina happily singing to herself as she set another place at the table. "By the way, please don't mention a baby again in front of your sister. She's having trouble enough getting used to her new surroundings. And to me," he added with a rueful smile.

Andreas regarded him, the sparkle gone from his eyes. His carefully tended mustache quivered with repressed emotion. "I am my sister's brother," he said. "I am ready to protect her with my life."

"I am, too," Adam replied. "Believe it!"

"Only if you promise to take good care of Melina. And only if I see my sister is happy."

"I will," Adam vowed. "Actually," he added, "I think I was about to make some progress along that line."

For a moment they stood eye to eye, man to man.

"Good!" Andreas finally said, although he didn't look satisfied. "You must promise to see to it Melina is happy here in your country, no?"

"Yes." Adam held out his hand and swallowed his smile at the not-so-veiled threat. Andreas might wear a suit and a tie, but he had the build of a stevedore and was clearly not a man to trifle with. He should have remembered Greek men were very protective of their women.

"If you're here because your father sent you to check up on your sister," Adam added, "you can tell him she's fine and that I intend to see to it that she stays that way. Now, come on in. Melina's made a great *avgolemono* and meatball soup for dinner. You should feel right at home."

Melina set a steaming bowl of soup in front of her brother and, smiling her pleasure, settled down at the table. "So tell me, little brother. What brings you here to San Francisco?"

Andreas avoided Adam's gaze and waved his spoon. "I am on my way to Los Angeles to consult with a former member of the 1984 Olympic committee. You see," he added modestly, "with my new degree in architecture, I have obtained a position on the staff of the Athens Olympic Committee."

Melina beamed. "Who would have thought you would be so successful, my little brother," she said proudly. "I remember you were a little boy I used to baby-sit, and now look at you! And, Christos? He is well?"

Andreas shrugged. "Christos has fallen in love with a girl he met at university. He has decided he has enough education and wants to get married and start a family. He intends to go into the family business with Papa. Although, what there is about pistachio trees to interest anyone... Anyway, Papa is pleased." He went back to his soup.

"And our mother and father?"

"They are well and send you their love."

Adam crossed his fingers and prayed the conversation would stick to family matters. Happily, Melina rushed to the kitchen and brought back a plate of *kourabiethes*.

"Your favorite cookies, Andreas," she said happily. "I baked them this afternoon. I must have sensed you would be coming here tonight. Now," she added briskly as she poured thick, black Greek coffee into demitasse cups. "How long can you stay with us?"

"No more than a few days, I am sorry." Andreas tasted a cookie and broke into a broad smile. "Ah, you bake just like our mother." He sipped his coffee and sat back. "I have appointments to keep in Los Angeles, but I will visit a few days with you on my return. That is, if you have room for me? If not I will go to a hotel."

"Of course not. Adam's little daughter, Jamie, is staying with her mother for a few days. You are welcome to her bed." Melina turned to Adam for approval. "No?"

"Yes," Adam said, by now used to the need to answer with an affirmative when the question sounded negative. If only he could read Melina's mind as easily as he had gotten used to her quaint use of English. Too bad Andreas had shown up at a time when he and Melina were about to resolve their misunderstanding.

His thoughts turned to the unhappy reminder he'd been sleeping in Jamie's bedroom for the past week.

He'd left enough evidence of his presence in the bedroom behind for Andreas to take notice.

What if Andreas put one and one together and decided there were big problems between himself and Melina? He eyed Andreas's broad shoulders and large hands. Architect or not, the outcome promised trouble.

Worse yet, had the INS been making inquiries in Athens about Melina? Was that why Andreas so conveniently stopped by? To warn her?

Considering that the seed of Melina's pregnancy had already been planted in Andreas's mind by his father, Adam decided to take on one problem at a time. He pushed the problem with the INS out of his mind for now.

"I'll go clear my stuff out of my daughter's bedroom... I've been sleeping there for the past few nights." When Andreas's eyebrows rose to meet in an arch, Adam tried to explain. "Melina hasn't been sleeping too well lately. I decided to give her some space."

Andreas sipped his coffee and rewarded his sister with a calculating smile. "Ah, so Papa was right, after all. You are not feeling well?" he said sympathetically.

Melina glanced at Adam, then frowned at her brother. "What is this thing you said when you came in? Papa told you I was expecting a baby? He is wrong!'' She glared at Adam. "This is what my father said before. It isn't true!''

Her brother looked bewildered. "Why are you so worried that I know about the baby, little sister? After all, you are a married woman now. Children are a blessing, or so our mother says.'' He chuckled and reached for another butter cookie. "Not that I am in a hurry for such blessings,'' he added wryly. "I leave the honor to Christos and to you and your husband.''

"What children are you still talking about?'' Melina asked ominously. "I told you, you are wrong! The only child here is Adam's daughter, Jamie.''

Andreas shrugged. "I don't think Papa meant that. That reminds me. Wait a minute.'' Andreas checked the pocket of his jacket. "Our mother gave me a list of natural herbs and foods for you to eat. She said to tell you they will settle your stomach and will keep the baby quiet and happy until it is born.''

Melina glared at her brother. "You are mad. I tell you again. There is no baby!''

Andreas grinned. "If you wish to keep it a secret, it is all right with me.''

Adam sensed the conversation was getting out of hand. It was time to break in. Although from the look on Melina's face, he was afraid he was already too late. Nothing he could say at this point would put out the fire growing in her eyes.

He tried concentrating on his soup, but he was very much aware that Melina was trying to hide her feelings. Under her chatter with her brother, he sensed there was a strong current of anger. She had to be biding her time to blow off steam. He just hoped it wasn't going to be at him.

Melina fixed Adam with a cold stare that sent chills running up and down his spine.

"It's not important, sweetheart. Besides, I think it's a little late to worry about who said what to whom. It might have started as a joke."

Melina's eyes narrowed.

"We'll speak of this later," Adam said, obviously responding to the grim look in her eyes. "Right now I think I'll get my things out of Jamie's room. Why don't you enjoy your visit with your brother? I'll be back in a few minutes."

With Andreas at the table, Melina knew she couldn't go further, but if what she suspected was true, Adam had gone through with their marriage only to protect her reputation. Her heart felt like a lump of lead in her chest.

She'd been on the verge of responding to Adam's attempt to reconcile, but no longer. There was no hope of him really loving her. He'd married her only to save her honor. The last thing she wanted from Adam was pity.

Andreas gazed wistfully at the butter cookies, then yawned and rose. "Excuse me. I'm afraid jet lag has finally caught up with me. I will go with your husband. We can talk later. Now, a kiss good night, eh?"

Melina turned her cheek for her brother's kiss, hoping he didn't notice the tears gathering in her eyes. Her brother's obvious love and affection were the only things she could be sure of. Adam had been so hot and cold toward her during their short marriage that her only defense was to harden her heart against him.

She cleared off the table. Only years of conditioned frugality prevented her from throwing away the uneaten soup—just as Adam had thrown away her love for him.

Adam came into view, carrying an armload of his clothing. After an apologetic glance, he disappeared into the master bedroom.

Melina cleared the table, put the dishes in the sink to soak and followed Adam. "Now is the time for this heart-to-heart!"

"Right. Now, before you go any further, I want to tell you you've got it all wrong. No matter how it sounded, I never meant to hurt you. Not before our marriage and not now."

"You already have," she said, her voice catching in her throat.

"Not true," Adam protested. "No matter how or why our marriage began, I meant it when I said I care for you."

Melina stoically met his gaze. She didn't care how he really felt about her, she told herself. As far as she was concerned, a marriage founded on lies was no marriage. As her mother had often told her, actions spoke louder than words.

"Your actions speak for you," she said softly. "As for the baby Andreas speaks of," she added in a deathly quiet voice, "it sounds as if my father actually believes I was compromised by you and had to get married. No?"

Adam tossed a small bundle of underwear in a dresser drawer and hung a suit in the clothes closet before he turned to face her. "You're right about your father, but you're wrong about me. Come on, Melina. I've changed. I'm not the man you met in Athens."

He tried to take her by her hand to get her to sit beside him on the bed. She stepped back and crossed her arms across her breasts. Maybe he shouldn't have used the word "joke."

"At the time we visited your parents, I gathered your father thought you were having a baby. And, worse yet, he thought it was mine. I know I should have set him straight right away, but I wasn't prepared to hang around and argue him out of the idea. He was too angry. I was also afraid of what he might say to you.''

''My father is very emotional,'' Melina. ''But you… When you said it was a joke, you knew what you were doing.''

''Sure. To be honest with you, I was anxious to get you out of there before he said something else to hurt you. I was hoping you didn't hear him. I already liked and respected you enough to go through with the marriage.''

''Was that why you were in such a hurry to marry me? You felt sorry for me?'' Her voice choked, there was a fire in her eyes that made his heart sink.

''No…. Maybe…. Not really.'' He ran his hands through his hair in his frustration. He was afraid if this argument kept up the way it was going, he'd lose her.

''Sure, I wanted to protect you,'' he went on. ''I wanted to keep you from being hurt. He gazed at her, a wry look on his face. ''But that's not the only reason I was in a hurry. I did have to get home to Jamie, I was telling the truth about that. It just all came together in a flash.''

He took a step toward Melina and reached for her hand. ''Believe me. I wanted you in my life.''

''Why?''

"Because you're honest. So loving and so lovely. When I'm around you I feel as if I'm walking on air. I guess you could say I've realized that with you in my life, my life has changed for the better.

"At first, the idea of having you in my life scared the hell out of me, it still does," he said with a crooked grin. "But I'm glad we decided to get married."

Melina backed away from his outstretched hand. "Don't speak to me as if I am a child, and do not call me sweetheart. I am a grown woman. I know when someone loves me. What you feel for me, and what you've shown me," she said with a sob in her voice, "is this thing called lust."

"Not true," Adam answered, desperate to take that cold look of loss out of her eyes. "My loving you that afternoon was a commitment. I only backed off when I realized I'd been your first lover because I didn't know how you actually felt about staying with me after Jamie leaves."

Melina shook her head and pointed to the sofa bed. "If that's all you have to say, *I* say that is where you will sleep tonight. Every night my brother is here and even when Jamie comes back to you."

Adam considered his chances of trying to talk Melina out of her anger. All things considered, he didn't blame her. But he had hoped to change her mind.

At the moment, he thought regretfully as he gazed at the tears that had gathered in the corner of her eyes, the chance of succeeding was slim to none.

What had started out to be his finest hour had turned into his darkest. Not even his breakup with his ex had affected him so much, except for his regret over the effect the divorce had had on Jamie. Jamie deserved better. He made up his mind that there wasn't going to be a second divorce, not only for Jamie's sake, but for his.

Trying to talk out their problems obviously wasn't enough to convince her that he'd loved her when he'd made love to her. Her literal-minded way of interpreting English into Greek had to be the reason why she'd misunderstood him. She didn't understand that he wanted more than to share the bed with her. The way he felt about her was deeper than he'd ever loved anyone.

Considering the look in her eyes, his chance of demonstrating his love would have to wait. A heart-to-heart was one thing, but how do you prove love to someone who doubts your every word?

ADAM SPENT a sleepless night on the sofa bed. Every nerve responded to Melina's sighs as she turned over in bed. He yearned to go to her, to show her how much he loved her, to end their estrangement. Too bad Andreas was in the next room.

He could hardly wait for tomorrow to come.

THINGS MIGHT HAVE GONE differently if only Melina's employer, Katherine Papadakis, hadn't shown up the next morning.

"You are well, my dear?" the woman asked when Melina opened the door to the town house. "I worried when you didn't show up for work this morning."

Adam hove into view at the sound of Katherine Papadakis's voice. "Katherine? What a surprise! Come on in. You're in time for coffee."

He regarded the woman he'd thought of as not only a good customer through the years, but also a good friend. It had been kind of her to employ Melina. Who else would give Melina a job when she was obviously so new to the country? And here without a green card?

"I missed your wife this morning," she answered with a quick look at Melina. "I locked up the store and came to see if she is well." She paused, then hesitantly asked, "You do not object to Melina helping me in the store?"

"I don't understand why Melina feels she has to earn her way," Adam said dryly as he glanced at his wife. "But no, I don't object. I was just surprised. I found out about her working for you by accident.''

Katherine Papadakis gasped. ''Accident? What accident? Where are you hurt?'' She reached for Melina and patted down her shoulders and arms.

Andreas strode out of his bedroom. ''Accident? What accident?'' He rushed over to Melina and eyed her carefully. ''Are you all right, Melina? Did the accident hurt the baby? Is that why you don't want to talk about it? Maybe you should be in bed!''

It was Adam's turn to gasp. After a sleepless night on the sofa bed with Melina an arm's reach away and yet untouchable, his nerves were already humming like a fine-tuned violin. Melina's ire was bad enough, but now the baby rumor was growing by leaps and bounds.

As was Melina's temper.

''There is no baby!'' Melina threw up her hands, turned on her heel and strode back into the living room. ''You are all mad!''

''Not me. I know better,'' Adam protested as he followed her. ''I've been trying to tell everyone so.''

Katherine trailed them into the room. ''What is this about a baby?''

''It is all a mistake, Katherine.'' Melina sank onto the couch and covered her eyes with shaking hands. ''I tell you, I am fine. I only remained home because my brother is here for a visit. There is no baby.''

"Let me look into your eyes, my dear." Katherine persisted after a worried look at Adam. "Maybe I can settle all of this for you."

"How can you settle something that doesn't exist?"

"Eyes never lie, my dear. Now, open your eyes and look at me."

Melina uncovered her eyes and glanced over at Adam.

"Go ahead and let Katherine look into your eyes," he advised. "Then we can all have a good laugh and put this rumor to rest once and for all."

Katherine muttered under her breath, put her purse on the coffee table and rolled up her sleeves. With an exasperated look at Adam, she took Melina's face between her hands and gazed deeply into her lavender eyes.

Melina tried hard not to blink, but her heart was beating wildly. How could she be pregnant after only one unplanned encounter with Adam? A man who had clearly shown he only lusted after her—even as she'd believed she was giving herself to her husband. A pregnancy would have been welcome if only her husband was a true husband. From the apprehensive look on his face, her baby was the last thing he wanted.

"I knew it! I am never wrong!" Katherine finally proclaimed. She pulled Melina into her arms and kissed her forehead. "So, when is the baby due, my dear?"

Behind her, Adam cursed softly under his breath. The woman might be well-intentioned, but she had to be wrong. No one could possibly predict a pregnancy by gazing into a woman's eyes. Besides, it was much too soon. It had only been a week or so since he'd made love to Melina.

*Without protection,* an inner voice reminded him.

Adam's blood ran cold. In the first place, he hadn't had protection with him that afternoon simply because he hadn't intended to make love to Melina—until the erotic statuary and the yearning look in Melina's glowing eyes had sent him over the edge.

In the second place, it had only been that one time.

Speechless, Adam watched while Katherine made soothing sounds to Melina.

Andreas glared at him. "You asked me to trust you, brother-in-law, yet you do not tell me the truth."

The fine hairs at the back of Adam's neck tingled. "I swear this comes as much a surprise to me as it does to you," he muttered as he glanced at the stunned look on Melina's face. A possible pregnancy obviously hadn't occurred to her, either.

In retrospect, he shouldn't have been surprised

she might be expecting. He'd been so deep in the throes of passion, his only thought, if he'd been thinking at all, had been how she apparently shared the wonderful moments of their joining.

One thing was damn sure. If Melina believed he'd taken advantage of her, any hope of a rapprochement between the two of them had turned into a pipe dream.

## Chapter Twelve

It had been a hellish two days.

Between trying to keep Andreas from worrying about his sister, and trying to make Melina happy, Adam felt as if he'd been walking a tightrope suspended between two sides of a steep abyss. Especially when Andreas didn't show signs of forgiving him for having made love to Melina and getting her pregnant. For that matter, neither did Melina.

He decided to knock off work early to show Melina and her brother something of the real San Francisco. And, not too coincidentally, to trade on Andreas's interest in architecture to keep Andreas happy while he was visiting.

"Did you know that the city of San Francisco was built on seven major hills?" Adam asked casually the next morning after breakfast.

"Like Rome?" Andreas's interest was caught. "Is there a place where we can see this?"

Bingo!

"Sure," Adam answered, pretending to think. A day of sight-seeing was obviously the answer to keep the guy occupied. "Got it! The hill that would probably be best, is Telegraph Hill. From the top, you can see for miles in all directions."

"Good. Let's go. Melina?"

"Melina, too, if she wants to. By the way, there are great examples of Californian Victorian architecture on the hill you might be interested in, including some of the so-called painted ladies. Maybe you've heard of them?"

Andreas nodded happily. "In books yes, but I would like to see them for myself."

"Good. Ready?"

"Is the hill really that high?" Melina asked worriedly.

"Yes, it is," Adam answered, taken aback at her reaction. From the fear on her face and in her eyes, it was obviously no idle question.

"Is something wrong?" Andreas asked. "Are you sure you feel well enough to come along with us?"

"Of course," she answered with a reassuring smile. She turned to Adam. "What is so interesting about this Telegraph Hill?"

"It was used as a signaling station during the nineteenth century. An electrical relay station re-

placed it later. Actually…'' Adam said, an eye on
Andreas, ''early immigrants to the United States settled there. Seems they still do.'' The more he explained the hill's history, the more Andreas came
alive. Even Melina began to look interested.

''Greek too?''

Adam grinned. ''Sure. They seem to love San
Francisco. When I was a kid,'' he went on, ''I used
to bicycle up to the top, look across to the Pacific
Ocean and pretend I was looking for pirate ships.
Unfortunately, there weren't any. When I grew
older, I even pictured myself taking a tramp steamer
I'd see in the bay and working my way around the
world. Guess that's one reason I eventually decided
to go into the foreign import business.''

Andreas's eyes lit up. ''We go up this hill today?''

''Sure,'' Adam agreed, ''only this time we can
take an elevator in the Coit Tower. From the top of
the tower, you'll have a 360-degree view of the city,
the bay and the Golden Gate Bridge. And, on a clear
day, you can see the Pacific Ocean.''

He caught sight of Melina, her tanned complexion
turning pale. ''Are you sure you want to come
along? We can make the tower before noon and still
have time for lunch afterward. Maybe enjoy some
freshly caught crabs down at the Wharf.''

To Adam's dismay, Melina's complexion paled

even more. His mind shot back to the time almost seven years before when Jeanette, expecting Jamie, had the same expression on her face. Whatever was wrong with Melina, he thought with alarm, it had to be a queasy stomach. "Maybe we can skip the crabs," he said hastily. "Ready?"

Thankfully, Coit Tower lived up to its reputation for its incomparable view. From its 179-foot height above the hill's summit, they gazed down the hillside. Adam pointed out quiet, wooded paths and the sites of some of the city's oldest homes. Below them, the sprawling city of San Francisco.

"Ah," Andreas said as he counted off the seven prominent hills listed in the guide brochure he'd picked up at the foot of the tower. "Your city is very interesting. Look at all that wonderful turn-of-the-century architecture! I will have to come back and visit you again. Eh, Melina?"

Melina hesitantly looked out over the horizon, paled and covered her lips with her hand. "I would like to go down now, please. I think I'm afraid of heights."

After a second look at Melina's drawn face, Adam had the uneasy feeling that her fear of heights masked something more—a pregnancy. His heart sank. He wanted children, but the timing stank. Could Katherine Papadakis have been right?

"Sure." He hurried to Melina's side. "You stay

up here, Andreas. We'll wait for you down below in the car.'' He put his arm around Melina's shoulders and guided her into the elevator. The small interior not only brought him closer to Melina than he'd been in the past two days, her scent was driving him up the wall. ''Are you sure you're okay?''

She took a deep swallow and held her middle as the elevator dropped to the first floor. ''I am sure. I think I am only a little tired. I'm afraid I didn't sleep too well the past few nights.''

Adam could relate to that statement. He hadn't slept more than a few hours, either. Still, his concern today was for Melina. He led the way to the parking lot.

''Tell you what. I'll take you back to the house so you can rest. Would you like me to stay with you?''

''No thanks,'' she said as she took a deep breath. ''It would be better if you stayed with Andreas. I will be fine.''

''All right,'' Adam said, reluctant to leave her at a time like this. ''I could take Andreas to see the painted ladies. Okay?''

She took another deep breath of fresh air. ''I will have dinner for you by the time you come home.''

''No way! You take a nap and forget about making dinner. I'll take Andreas to a great fish house down at the wharf. Promise?''

Melina swallowed hard. "Thank you. I am sorry to upset your plans. I will have to apologize to my brother when you come home."

Adam fought back his own need to apologize. Not only for making unprotected love to her, but for his stupid reaction to the unexpected prospect of fatherhood. He wanted to tell her that his only excuse was that he hadn't planned ahead to make love to her. To tell her that her quaint sweetness and innate sensual appeal had gotten to him. And, maybe, because he'd already thought of her as his wife.

Perhaps this wasn't the time or the place to bare his heart. Every time he tried to explain how he felt about her, he seemed to put his foot into it. Hell, she'd even been offended when he'd apologized after making love to her before, when all he was trying to do was to explain he hadn't planned on breaking their bargain.

Given time, they would have had that talk, and he would have told her how much he respected and had grown to love her.

She hadn't waited long enough for him to gather his thoughts together before she'd clammed up. Didn't she know that it wasn't easy for a man to bare his soul?

The proof she thought he had rejected her as a wife was in the way their relationship had gone downhill ever since.

THE DAYS PASSED with Melina taking afternoon naps while Adam and Andreas visited every old building and private residence Andreas found in the local tourist guidebook.

On the third day, when it came time for Andreas to leave, he pulled Adam aside. "I must say good-bye for now, but I will stop here on my way home to Greece," Andreas said in quiet undertones when he and Adam were alone. "You will see to it my sister has a smile on her face instead of tears in her eyes when I return?"

Adam swallowed hard. "Right. I'm sure this thing about a baby is all a misunderstanding. I honestly don't believe that Mrs. Papadakis could know Melina is expecting a baby. It's too soon."

"Some Greek women have second sight," Andreas mused out loud as he gazed at the kitchen where Melina was rummaging in the pantry. "My own mother is one of those women. Too bad she's not here to help my sister through this. You promise you will take care of Melina?"

"I've already sworn that I will." Adam glanced over to where Melina was packing cookies in a small plastic container for Andreas to take with him. "Don't worry. My reaction to the news about the baby, if true, was that I was taken by surprise. Once I convince Melina I'm happy to be a father again, I'm sure everything will be okay."

"You were surprised to find your wife expecting a baby?" Andreas frowned at the thought. "My sister was an innocent when she married you, even I, as part of her family, knew that. But you are her husband," he said accusingly. "If you didn't want a child, you should have known better."

Adam shrugged helplessly. "I'm trying to tell you that no matter how it looks, I want this baby. Melina thinks I don't, but I'm telling you I do. I would love a child of ours as I love your sister."

Andreas's hard look mellowed a bit, but he didn't look convinced. "I will return in two days," he said as he started toward the kitchen.

Adam hung back. To his dismay, the news sounded more like a threat than a promise.

Adam watched as Andreas hugged his sister and said goodbye. After the young man's veiled threat, he was sure that whatever Andreas was saying to her was more than a simple goodbye. Especially when Melina glanced his way before she nodded.

Adam was willing to bet his right arm Andreas had offered to take her back to Greece with him on his way home if she wanted to go.

The idea Melina might actually decide to go back to Greece in a few days began to scare the hell out of Adam. He couldn't lose her now. She'd not only changed his life, she filled a void he hadn't even been aware was there until after he'd met, married her and brought her home to San Francisco.

One thought led to another. He, who had sworn never to love again, let alone to remarry, had not only fallen for Melina like a ton of bricks, but could be about to become a father again. Considering his earlier unhappy experience as a husband, both events were nothing short of a miracle.

But one thing was damn sure, Andreas Kostos or not, he didn't intend to let Melina go back to Greece without trying to convince her that he'd grown to love her and wanted her to stay with him forever.

As far as a baby was concerned, if Katherine Papadakis was wrong and Melina *wasn't* carrying his child, he still didn't intend to let Melina go. Marriage of convenience or not, she was his wife and belonged here with him.

As far as the baby went, as Jamie's part-time father, he'd learned a hard lesson he never intended to repeat. This time, he was going to be a full-time husband and a full-time father.

The answer to his problem was clear. He'd have to stop worrying about honoring that damn fool bargain. A bargain Melina clearly had come to regret. He'd have to begin acting like a believable, loving husband. He'd have to bite the bullet, court Melina and get her to marry him again. This time, in deference to her wishes, with the whole nine yards of the traditional Greek wedding she'd dreamed of, including her family.

He'd show her he cared for her instead of just talking about it. From what he'd come to realize about Melina and her dreams, nothing less would keep her here.

One thing he was damn sure about, he thought with relief, was that Melina was so responsible she would never break her word to stay with him as long as she thought he needed her.

Needed Melina? He wanted her! She was lovely, passionate and worthy of being loved.

He wanted his wife back. A real wife.

MELINA SURVEYED THE BED where Andreas had slept during his visit. The idea that Adam would sleep here again now that her brother was leaving troubled her more than she was willing to admit.

Her heart softened as she recalled what Adam had said about bicycling up Telegraph Hill to look out over the bay. She envisioned him as a little boy dreaming of pirates and traveling to faraway places. Then later, becoming strong and resourceful enough to turn those dreams into an exotic business of his own.

She'd had her dreams, too. As a child she'd dreamed of visiting the United States she'd studied in school. Her venture into working at the American embassy in Athens hadn't come with her father's approval, but she'd done it anyway. Now that she'd foolishly married Adam to make that dream come true, she'd probably alienated the father she loved in the process.

She might be a fool, she mused as her thoughts turned back to Adam. In spite of Adam's behavior, she'd managed to fall in love with him. She yearned to have him in bed beside her at night instead of sleeping alone. His gaze meeting hers while they shared unspoken thoughts. She ached to have him take her in his arms and to make the exquisite love to her that he'd made to her a short while ago.

When had everything gone wrong between herself and Adam? she wondered sleepily as she gazed at the bed. Should she stick out her bargain or should she take her brother up on his offer to see her home to Greece and into her mother's loving arms?

Weary, she finally dropped down on the newly changed bed to feel nearer to Adam. She closed her eyes, drifted off to sleep and imagined herself back in that wondrous afternoon when she had unexpectedly become a woman in Adam's arms.

From the moment she'd turned her fascinated gaze from the erotic Greek statuary in Adam's warehouse to meet his sensuous, warm eyes, she'd known he wanted her as a man wants a woman. Just as she wanted him. Without pretense and without any artificial barriers between them. His very glance had warmed her. Warmed her until she'd felt the stirring of a desire she'd carefully tried to ignore. When he'd gazed at her with longing in his eyes, she hadn't stopped to think. She'd wanted to make love with him with every ounce of the love burning within her. There, in the place where the scents and sights from her homeland had reawakened her dreams, and where the man she loved beckoned her, she'd given in to her deepest desires.

In the process, instead of gaining Adam as a true husband, she had managed to lose him.

Half asleep, she heard footsteps approach the bed. She felt Adam's arms around her once again, soothing and stroking her skin. She reveled in the sound of his low, sensuous voice murmuring love words in her ear as he moved to lie beside her. She felt his warm, work-roughened hands reach behind her to gently loosen her bra, then move on to slide her blouse away from her shoulders. His warm breath drifted over her skin as he caressed her shoulders and cupped her breasts. Smiling, she inhaled again his faint spicy scent that took her back to that afternoon when she'd lost her innocence.

Wave after wave of mind-shattering sensations swept over her when he bent to tongue her aching breasts. Lost in the mystical and magical moments, she moaned when he slid his hands down her sensitive skin to her waist and then slowly moved on to even more sensitive spots. She arched into his arms, inviting more intimate caresses, but, just when a warmth began to cover her, he stopped and pulled away.

She frowned. "Adam?"

"Shush, sweetheart," Adams low voice said. "Go back to sleep now. I'll be here when you awaken."

Melina tried to awaken…if only she didn't feel overcome by the need to sleep! If this was a dream, and the only way she could be a true wife to Adam as she yearned to be, she didn't want him to stop. She wanted the precious and magical moments between them that were sending her soaring to last forever.

*"S'agapo, agapee mou,"* she murmured and held out her arms for Adam to take him to her aching breasts. "I love you, my husband."

She held her breath, waiting for his reply. Waiting for him to take her in his arms and to finish what he'd started.

Even as she reached for him, his image dimmed. "Go to sleep, sweetheart," he whispered. "I'll be here when you wake up."

How real it had all seemed, Melina thought as she

sighed with unfulfilled longings. Longings only her husband had awakened and only her husband could fill.

She sighed and turned over to find a more comfortable place for herself in the bed. "Later," she agreed as she fell into a deep sleep.

ADAM SILENTLY ROSE from the bed before he lost control of himself. Before he took Melina in his arms, awakened her and showed her just how real he was. Although, he mused as he stood gazing down at her exquisite sleeping form, he was sure he'd learned what he'd wanted to know. Awake, Melina might not want to admit the truth…she loved him.

He leaned over and tenderly pulled a tendril of her silky hair away from her closed eyes. To his surprise, she turned her face into his hand and pressed a kiss into it.

She had to love him, Adam thought again. His heart warmed, his spirits soared. Maybe they didn't have to talk, after all. Maybe all he had to do was show her how much he loved her. Until he noticed unshed tears at the corners of her eyes.

Tears? At a time she appeared to be so content, so loving, so happy?

The truth hit him square in his gut. Melina was able to say she loved him only in her sleep! Asleep, she kissed his hand. Awake, she acted as if he'd betrayed her.

Was it because she *did* feel betrayed?

Was it because she didn't want his child?

Was it because she hadn't been able to find a way to tell him how she felt about him?

Is that why the tears?

That was okay with him, he thought bitterly as he straightened and turned away from the bed. He'd planned to ask her for another chance when she awakened. A chance to show her that the foolish bargain they'd entered should never have been made in the first place. Not when he must have known that he, a single, red-blooded man and Melina a single, red-blooded woman, would be attracted to each other.

Melina's brother had been right about him. He was the one with experience. He should have known better than to make love to Melina that afternoon without protection.

He called himself all kinds of a fool for planning to ask Melina for a chance to start all over again. To ask her to enter a relationship where touching in private would consume all their waking hours. To forget that heart-to-heart. To demand the truth about how she felt about him and what she wanted to do with her life. Once and for all, and before it was too late.

He couldn't force Melina to love him, he thought as he turned to leave the bedroom. If she was carrying their child, he intended to insist she remain with him instead of returning to Greece with Andreas. She belonged with him, the man who loved her, the father of her child.

He started back to awaken her, then stopped. She looked so sweet, so innocent lying there with her arms curled around a pillow, she managed to touch some cold place in his heart.

He'd let Melina sleep for now, but he intended to show her how much he loved her before another day passed.

## Chapter Thirteen

When Melina finally awakened the next morning, the sun was shining through the bedroom curtains. To her regret, instead of finding herself in her own bedroom, she was in Jamie's bed. Instead of finding the warmth of Adam's body, her arms were curled around a pillow.

It took her a few moments to realize she'd fallen asleep from exhaustion and had slept through the night. A night when her yearning had seemed so real, she'd actually felt Adam's arms around her. Had it only been a dream?

How could it have been a dream when she remembered the way he had caressed her bare skin?

How could it have been a dream when she remembered the sweet sensations his hard lips and seeking hands had sent spiraling through her?

When she remembered his low, magnetic voice

whispering love words into her ear as he nipped at the sensitive spot on the back of her neck?

If it had been real, how could he have left her after she'd shown him how much she ached to have him join his body with hers again? How could he have left her with empty arms? Without a word of regret and without even a goodbye?

She glanced around the room to where Jamie's favorite teddy bear sat on a rocking chair soulfully gazing back at her. The bear's wise eyes seemed to be telling her she was on her own. He was alone and forgotten, too.

The bear was a stuffed animal, subject to Jamie's whim. But she was a grown woman with a mind of her own. Clearly, the decision whether to stay or to leave was up to her.

Her heart told her to stay to try to become Adam's true wife and the mother of his children. Her head told her to leave to seek a new life for herself.

She had to face the truth. Last night *had* been a dream, wishful thinking or a sexual fantasy. The truth had to be that Adam might want her as a man wants a desirable woman, but he hadn't wanted her as a wife.

Disappointed, her heart aching until she thought it would break in two, Melina threw off the blanket that covered her and slid out of bed. She'd made a decision. With Jamie out of the picture, she no longer had a reason to remain with Adam. She'd made her independent way in the world before and she'd do it again.

DETERMINED TO SHOW Melina how much he cared for her, now that they were finally alone, Adam left his foreman in charge of the warehouse and made for home. Now was the perfect time to settle anything wrong between them, he told himself as he made his way through traffic.

The more he thought of it, the more he was sure that the only thing that stood between them was a series of misunderstandings. Surely they would be able to agree they were meant for each other. All he needed was a few uninterrupted moments alone with her.

"Melina!" he called as he came in the door. When there was no answer, he went from room to room looking for her. His heart began to pound when he realized there was no sign of Melina cooking up a storm, or signs of a table set for a romantic dinner. No sound of Melina singing softly to herself. Not even a note on the table telling him where she'd gone.

Alarmed, a mental picture formed in his mind. His first wife had said he never noticed her, but with Melina, Adam noticed everything.

Before she'd disappeared into Jamie's room to

change the bed last night, he remembered seeing Melina fold newly laundered clothing into two separate piles. Had she been getting ready to pack?

He strode back to their bedroom. Sure enough, Melina's overnight case and one of her suitcases were missing.

Cold chills ran over him. He'd been right. After he'd watched her sleeping and seen the tears at the corners of her eyelashes he should have known she'd already decided to leave him.

How stupid he'd been for walking away when he should have taken her in his arms and changed her mind then and there! He should have joined Melina in that single bed last night. Scarcely wide enough to have held the both of them while he made love to her, they would have been eye to eye, lip to lip, and at least forced to share their feelings about each other.

His only excuse was that she'd looked so exhausted he hadn't had the heart to awaken her long enough to show her that he loved her for the wonderful woman she was and not for only her exquisite body.

Even so, he hadn't been able to turn away from her without giving in to his need to at least touch her. He quietly thanked his lucky star at having found a nurturing, loving and enchanting woman from a country he loved almost as much as he did his own. A precious woman he'd grown to love and who surely returned his love. Who else would have made that journey from a life she'd known to journey thousands of miles away, and with a stranger?

He went back to Jamie's room and stood in the doorway looking for some clue as to where Melina had gone—at least a note? The bed was freshly made, the light blanket he'd thrown over Melina last night as she'd slept neatly folded at the foot of the bed. The only possible sign of Melina's turmoil was Jamie's teddy bear lying facedown in the middle of the empty bed.

He lingered beside the bed and thought of the way Melina had murmured in her sleep that she loved him. Of the way her silken skin slid under his fingers when he'd given in to the need to at least touch her, to feel her heartbeat before he'd left her to her dreams.

He thought of the way she'd held out her hands, inviting him to take her in his arms and to make love to her again. Fool that he had been, he'd decided to wait until morning. Now it might be too late.

Cold waves of fear covered him as he thought of the missing suitcases. No matter what endearments she'd said to him in her sleep, awake she must have determined to end what she must have decided was an ill-fated marriage.

After turning away from the tears lurking at the corners of her eyes last night, he shouldn't be surprised to find her gone this morning.

But where?

Had Andreas returned earlier than planned and taken her back to Greece with him? Could they have made the agreement before her brother had left for Los Angeles?

Adam paced the floor. He glanced at his watch. Ten minutes later, he checked again.

And then the doorbell rang, followed by an impatient knock.

Adam threw open the door.

A telegraph messenger handed him a telegram. Andreas telling him he'd been delayed in Los Angeles and would be coming in late tonight or tomorrow morning.

Adam breathed a sigh of relief. At least Melina hadn't already gone home to Greece with her brother. She had to still be here in San Francisco.

He sensed he didn't have time to waste. There was no doubt in his mind that Melina had decided to leave him. Without a friend in San Francisco, where would she go?

To Katherine Papadakis! A woman who, in a short space of time, had become Melina's friend? Who better than a person who was clearly fond of her to tell her troubles to? Or, if Melina had decided to remain in the United States, who better to ask for work so she could remain here?

His heart sank. It wasn't only his finding her that Melina had to consider. She didn't know the lengths to which the immigration service would go to find her if they suspected them of fraud.

Thirty minutes later, Katherine Papadakis peered at Adam. "What do you mean, Melina is gone from home?" she shouted. "She is lost? Have you called the police?"

"Lost? I don't know." Adam struggled to control his temper. "Like I said, I came home an hour ago to find her gone. I figured she might be here with you." Adam looked over the woman's shoulder. Behind her, a dozen women shopping in the grocery store, all of them covertly attracted by the storekeeper's loud question.

"No, the poor girl called this morning to tell me she wouldn't be back to work. Who else does she know in San Francisco?"

Adam shook his head. Given the opportunity, he would have spoken his mind about the role Katherine Papadakis had played in Melina's disappearance—especially for predicting an unexpected baby. As she was the only Greek-speaking person Melina knew, Adam figured he'd better play it cool. As for Melina being a girl…enough of that. His missing wife was definitely a grown woman, queasy stomach and all.

Adam edged toward the storeroom at the back of the store and glanced inside. If Melina was hiding anywhere near, it wasn't there. "I haven't a clue," he said, raking his fingers through his hair in his frustration. "She's vanished into thin air without a word. I don't even know where to begin to look for her."

Storm signals filled the woman's eyes. Her black eyebrows rose until they came together. "Ah! What did you say to the child to make her leave you like that?"

"It's more what I didn't say," Adam replied, one foot out the door. "I'm sorry, I have to go."

Mrs. Papadakis crossed herself and rolled her eyes toward the ceiling. "Men! All talk!" She shook her finger. "Go, find your sweet wife. When you do find her, no more talk! We Greek women want action. Show her how you feel about her!"

"I will," Adam replied fervently.

"Be sure to let me know when you find her!" Katherine called after him. "Remember, no more talk!"

Adam waved his hand as he strode to his car. In the first place, if he knew where Melina had gone, he would have brought her home by now. In the second place, he wouldn't have wasted any more time talking.

Not at first, anyway. Maybe later. After he'd shown Melina how much he loved her.

He headed for the San Francisco International Airport, cursing as the freeway traffic crawled along. It looked as if half of San Francisco was heading south to the airport and the other half returning home.

Half an hour later, he turned over his car to a parking attendant and ran for the Delta Air Lines terminal, the airline Andreas had mentioned he'd taken from Greece.

Red warning signs shouted that no one would be allowed beyond the ticket counter. He was considering his options and striding through the crowd when he noticed a uniformed guard eyeing him warily. He stepped up his pace, looking for Melina. She might be waiting for her brother and couldn't have possibly known Andreas was delayed.

He had to stop her before she gave up waiting and disappeared into the night or he'd never be able to find her. He had to somehow convince her to come home with him. To at least give him a chance to explain.

He thought of Katherine Papadakis's last words. *No more talking!* Okay, he silently agreed as he continued to search the milling crowds. But only after he'd had a chance to tell Melina he loved her and wanted her, baby and all.

He was about to ask an airport security guard to page Melina when he saw her coming out of a women's room. To his relief, awkwardly clutching her baggage, she was headed for the computerized board announcing incoming flight information.

"Melina!" he called, rushing after her. "Wait up!"

She turned at his call, tossed her head as if to dismiss him and planted herself in front of the board.

"Go away," she said when he pulled up at her side. "I love the United States, but between the immigration service and you, I do not feel welcome here. When my brother arrives, I will consider going home to Greece with him."

"Home is here with me, Melina," he said. "For you and our baby." He took her elbow and tried to turn her around to face him. Talking might be out, but, thank God, according to their bargain, touching in public was okay.

"Home is Nafplion!" she said and tried to pull away. "At least there, in the village of my ancestors, I know I am welcome and wanted."

"Forget Nafplion. *I* want you, sweetheart." Short of taking her in his arms in public, Adam put every ounce of love he could muster into his voice.

"As a man who wants a woman," she said scornfully. "That is all I am to you."

"No. I promise you, you have it all wrong. I want you as a man wants the woman he loves and the woman he wants to spend the rest of his life with. Don't you ever doubt it!"

The couple standing beside Melina swung around at Adam's declaration. The woman gazed at Adam, sighed and poked her husband. "Why can't you say such beautiful things to me, Robert, instead of taking me for granted?"

The man scowled at Adam. "If this is a pickup, the lady doesn't appear to be willing. You'd better get lost before you cause any more trouble. If you don't, I'm going to call the guards."

An uniformed airport policeman moved up alongside Melina and glanced at Adam. "Is this man bothering you, miss?"

"She's not a miss, she's a missus." Adam put his arm around Melina. "She's my wife."

"Maybe so, but she's still free to come and go as she pleases. It sounds to me like she wants to leave. Ma'am?" he asked as he reached for a set of handcuffs at his belt.

Melina froze. The last thing she wanted was for Adam to be arrested and taken off to jail. Where, heaven forbid, the truth about their relationship could come out. Getting married for convenience was surely legal and nothing new, but how many convenient brides had applied for a green card?

Her thoughts swung wildly. Adam was a prominent businessman, a father. What if the newspapers picked up on his arrest? Everything he represented and everything he worked for would surely be lost if he were charged with the crime of bringing her into his country under false pretenses.

She couldn't do that to him. In spite of his having broken her heart, she loved him too much. His only crime was in not loving her.

As for meeting her brother, becoming involved in a police affair was the last thing he needed.

"I'm sorry to have bothered you, Officer," she said. She dropped her suitcases and sent the man a wistful smile. "I'm afraid I lost my temper with my husband and was trying to punish him. The truth is—" she pointed to her purse "—I don't actually have the money to buy a ticket. I was hoping my husband would come after me." She dimpled.

The officer dropped his hand. "Well, if that's all it was…. For the record, ma'am, please try to remember that these days we take any disturbance seriously. Next time, things might end in a way you wouldn't like." He paused and peered at Melina. "Are you sure it was only a family misunderstanding? Do you really want to go home with him?"

Melina picked up her luggage and thrust it at

Adam. She had to get out of the airport before the guard changed his mind and arrested Adam. "I do." She leaned over and whispered in the man's ear, "Pregnancy always makes me a little, what you call, emotional."

The frown on the guard face disappeared. "Yeah, I've been there several times myself. Ought to have recognized the symptoms." He turned to Adam. "If I were you, I'd take the little lady home and rub her feet. Never fails to soften 'em up, makes 'em relax."

To Melina's relief, Adam played along. He dropped a suitcase and reached for the guard's hand. "Thanks. Guess I wasn't thinking clearly. This is our fourth kid. I should have remembered that," he said as he shook the man's hand fervently. He turned to her. "Ready to go home now, sweetheart?"

Melina smiled her apologies to her interested and envious female audience. "I am ready, my husband."

Adam silently led the way to the parking curb where he gave his parking ticket to an attendant. Melina settled into the seat. She eyed Adam's tense expression as he glanced through the rearview mirror and steered the car into terminal traffic. How could she be angry with him when she was at fault for letting her pride come between them? For not sharing the words her heart was saying?

She put her hand on his knee to show him she

was pleased he had come to find her. "You have something to tell me, no?"

He glanced over at her, his expression softening. "Actually, a lot of something not only to tell you but to show you," he said. "It's just a little difficult to do it until we get home."

She waited until they finally pulled up in front of the town house. "I, too, have something to tell you."

She followed him inside. "We talk now?"

"Later." He dropped her suitcases, locked the door behind him and smiled at her. "First, I believe we have something to settle between us."

At the heated look that came into his eyes, butterflies began to careen through Melina's stomach. When he took a step toward her, his eyes darkening with desire, she recognized the feeling. It was the same ache that had swept through her last night and was sweeping through her now.

How could she tell him that she couldn't let him touch her? How could she still keep her distance from him?

"No more talk," he said warmly as he reached for her and pulled her into his arms. "Maybe trying to talk things out was our problem. I think we need to forget talking." He lifted her chin with a tender forefinger and bent to graze her parted lips with his own. "Maybe this is the kind of talking we do best, anyway. Anything else can wait. Right?"

"Yes," she agreed as she gazed into his warm eyes. "Our most precious moments were filled with action, not words. Let me show you how much I love you."

With a low growl of pleasure, Adam pulled her closer, kissed the corners of her eyes, one by one, then held her closer still. "Your bed or mine?"

"Ours," she whispered against his hard lips. When Adam picked her up and strode into their bedroom, she almost wept with pleasure.

She pulled at his clothing. "I want to see you. All of you. I want to touch your skin as you once touched mine."

Adam laughed. "My very proper little Greek wife." He stood her on her feet and murmured into her neck, "You've sure changed."

"I think it is you who have changed," she said as he tugged off her blouse and kissed his way across her shoulders and down to her breasts.

"You're right," Adam murmured into the hollow between her breasts. "I've opened my heart to the possibility I could be a good husband and a good father. But only with you as my wife."

"Perhaps I have changed, too," she added as he nipped at her. "It is good, no?"

"It is good, yes. But I would prefer you stay as

sweet as you are." Adam reached behind her to undo her bra. "Very good."

"Wait," she said before he could peel off the rest of her clothing. "We cannot do this now. Andreas will be coming soon."

Adam grinned. "Not for hours, and maybe not even tonight. He sent a telegram when he couldn't reach us. His flight has been delayed."

"In that case, come to bed, my husband," she said with a happy smile. "It is time to start again."

Her heart turned over when Adam silenced her with a kiss, lifted her in his arms and set her on the bed. This time there were no spicy foreign scents or erotic statuary to use as an excuse for igniting their desire for each other. This time, it was Adam and his sensual touch and telling glance that set her on fire.

"I love you," she murmured as they undressed each other. "I think I have loved you from the day we met. I just didn't have the experience to recognize the feeling."

"Me, too," Adam said fervently as he bent to kiss her at the fold of her breast. "Remind me to thank Peter Stakis for introducing us that day at the embassy."

Melina opened her arms to him, inviting him to ease the ache that filled her. Inviting him to let her ease the ache she saw in his eyes. "Love me, my husband."

To her delight, Adam came into her arms and slowly, sensuously, made her heart sing with joy.

Finally sated, Melina curled into Adam's embrace. In spite of her delight and deep pleasure at the heights to which Adam had taken her, she felt as if there was something about their marriage still lacking. She wouldn't feel truly married until the void was filled. She sighed against his bare shoulder.

"Something still bothering you, sweetheart?" Adam murmured as he grazed her cheek with the back of his hand. "Come on, out with it."

"I'm afraid I don't feel as if we are truly man and wife," she confessed. "Something is missing."

He pulled away and stared at her. "Not even after the wedding ceremony at the American embassy? If that's what's bothering you, I swear it was a legal wedding. I have a marriage certificate to prove it."

Trying to still her runaway emotions, Melina gazed at him. "I know. You are not the one at fault for my not feeling truly a wife. It's just that I should have asked you to wait until we could have a proper Greek wedding."

Adam sat up, propped himself against the headboard and settled her in his arms. "Are you sure that's all that's troubling you?"

"The baby," she murmured. "If there is to be a

child, the three of us must be blessed in a proper Greek wedding for our union to be complete.''

Adam sat silently for a long moment. She was beginning to see that his silences were for deep thought, unlike her father's where silences always meant anger. ''Is that a problem for you?''

''No.'' He wound a strand of her hair around his fingers and brought it to his lips. ''I was just thinking about what your father would say if I approached him about coming over here for a second wedding.''

''I think he would be pleased to see us married in a real Greek wedding.''

Adam grinned. ''I'd love that, too, sweetheart. We'll go over to the Greek cathedral and make the arrangements. And, now that that's taken care of…'' He slipped down into the rumpled bed with Melina in his arms. ''No more talking. I made a promise to someone to show you how much I love you.''

And he did.

## Epilogue

Three weeks later Adam stood in the chapel of San Francisco's beautiful Greek cathedral waiting for the second and this time, proper, wedding to begin. His lovely Greek bride had been right. He was beginning to feel like a real bridegroom, and the ceremony hadn't even begun!

The sweet scent of the floral canopy under which he and Melina were to exchange their marriage vows filled the air. The two floral wreaths he understood would be held above his and Melina's heads as they walked around the altar were waiting.

"How did you manage to persuade Melina's parents and brothers to come over here?" Peter Stakis, Adam's best man, asked. "Knowing Kostos, I would have thought he would insist you get married in their family church.

"And by the way," Peter said as he anxiously checked in his side pocket for the sixth time for the wedding rings, "I hope you don't intend to make a practice of getting remarried every few months, my friend. I hate being in an airplane."

"Melina insisted. Says she thinks of herself as a Greek American. As for her parents being here, she didn't feel our first wedding at the embassy was real without them there," Adam said with a wry smile. "Convincing her father to come here and to bring the family wasn't easy. The poor man protested up a storm—until Melina gently reminded him of his future grandchild."

Peter's eyebrows rose. "Grandchild? Already?" He eyed Adam. "I thought you and Melina met in the elevator at your embassy. Maybe I misunderstood. Maybe you had already met and were playing a game."

"Nope," Adam said with a grin, "you're right. The first time we met was in the elevator."

Peter laughed. "No wonder Mikis Kostos was furious when you showed up two days later engaged to his daughter. You don't fit the mold of a proper Greek son-in-law. But already a baby!"

"There was no baby, at least not at that time," Adam said bluntly. "You have my word on it. Her father had it all wrong—damn near broke Melina's heart."

Peter glanced over to where Mikis Kostos was talking with the priest. "My pardon, my friend. I've always believed Melina a lady.'' He winked at Adam. ''By the time Kostos satisfies himself that the priest knows what he is doing, the man will come around. Children are very welcome in our culture.''

''Mine, too, I just didn't expect to become a father again so soon.'' Adam glanced over to the few seats filled with the Papadakis clan and the various Greek friends he'd made through the years and rubbed his finger under his suddenly too tight tuxedo shirt collar. ''Wish we'd get this shindig started,'' he muttered.

As he spoke four men with clarinets and bouzoukis in an adjoining hall burst into music. The two bridesmaids—Eleni and Arianna who Adam had flown in from Greece as a wedding present to Melina—got in line. The two ushers—Melina's two brothers—joined them.

The bride, his beautiful and unique Greek wife, emerged from behind a screen where her mother, Anna Kostos, had insisted she hide from Adam until she walked down the aisle. A good-luck thing, she'd said.

Adam hid a grin. The Kostos family were playing the wedding as if he and Melina were getting married for the first time. He was willing to play it any way Anna Kostos wanted. Anything to see the sparkle in his bride's eyes. Even if he had to marry her in every country in Europe to convince her that he meant it when he said he loved her.

After all, he thought as he watched Melina's parents take her by her arms, he'd seen his bride in a wedding dress before, and—he breathed a guilty but pleased sigh—in a lot less. Each time he looked at Melina, he realized how lucky he was for their having met. Never before, and never again, he thought as Melina raised her head and smiled at him, would he see a lovelier woman than the way his wife looked today.

"Looks like it's time to begin, thank God." Peter Stakis straightened and sniffed at the tantalizing scent of Greek cooking that floated in from the social hall. "I'm starved. Knowing Anna Kostos probably did most of the cooking doesn't make it any easier for me to wait."

Adam gazed at his father-in-law, who now stood at Melina's side with a wide smile on his face. He should have known Melina's father loved her as much as Adam did.

Two by two, the wedding party made its way down the aisle. After a flourish from the clarinets, a small figure in a white, organdy, ankle-length dress with rosebuds in her hair started down the aisle in front of the bride.

Adam smiled proudly. In her miniature bride dress, his little Jamie looked as if she'd walked out of a dream. Young now, but growing up too fast, he thought with another sigh. For the first time Adam understood his father-in-law's reaction when Adam and Melina had announced they were getting married—without her parents' consent and without waiting for a full-blown wedding. A man would have wanted to protect his daughter.

By the time Melina reached his side and placed her hand in his, Adam had a lump in his throat. Instead of the wary look she'd had on her face the first time they'd exchanged marriage vows, today his bride had a trusting smile on her face.

"Thank you for doing this for me, my husband," she whispered.

"You're welcome, my wife," Adam replied. Heck, the Greek ceremony was easy. He would have given her the moon if she'd asked for it.

"Dearly beloved, we are gathered here today to join this man and woman in holy matrimony," the priest solemnly began.

MELINA LOST TRACK of the ceremony and began to feel uneasy when she felt her mother's form press against her back. It was the custom for those standing under the wedding canopy with the bride and groom to share in the final blessings, but this was too much.

She glanced up at the canopy. It was wide enough

to cover her and Adam, perhaps even her parents, but she feared for the outcome if her mother continued to drag in relatives.

Melina held her breath and tried to concentrate on the ceremony. She glanced up at Adam and met his sympathetic gaze. She bit her lower lip, reached for his hand and held on tight. But at least she would remember she and Adam making their wedding vows.

Between her mother pulling relatives under the canopy for the final blessing, and her father's muttered complaints about the wedding not being held in the main cathedral, the ceremony passed in a haze.

Pushed out from under the floral canopy by her well-meaning mother, her wedding veil pushed over her eyes, the only way Melina knew she and Adam had actually gotten married was through Adam's tight hold on her hand.

When the priest said, "You may kiss the bride," Adam pulled her against him and kissed her eyes, her lips. Behind him he heard Anna Kostos weep with joy.

"Never again," he whispered as the small band in the social hall began to play a lively wedding dance and shouts of *"Hopa!"* filled the air.

"I hope you agree this time is for real, sweetheart," Adam managed to whisper before Melina could be torn from his grasp to be carried away to join the line of dancers. "No more foolish bargains. Now we get to touch each other both in public and in private," he added with a tender smile as he traced her lips with a finger. "I don't know about you, sweetheart, but I can hardly wait to get you alone."

Melina smiled over her shoulder before she disappeared into the crowd. "And I can't wait for you to get me alone, my love."

## *Forrester Square*
### LEGACIES . LIES . LOVE .

### July 19, 1983...

The Kinards, the Richardses and the Webbers—Seattle's
Kennedys. Their "compound"—elegant Forrester Square...
until the fateful night that tore these families apart.

### Twenty years later...

Their children were reunited. Repressed memories and
family secrets were about to be revealed. And one person
was out to make sure they never remembered...

# Save $1.00 off
## your purchase of any
## Harlequin® Forrester Square title
## on-sale August 2003 through July 2004

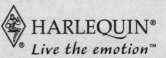

5 65373 00076 2     (8100)0 11105

## HARLEQUIN®
### *Live the emotion*™

## *Forrester Square*

### LEGACIES . LIES . LOVE .

## July 19, 1983…

The Kinards, the Richardses and the Webbers—Seattle's
Kennedys. Their "compound"—elegant Forrester Square…
until the fateful night that tore these families apart.

## Twenty years later…

Their children were reunited. Repressed memories and
family secrets were about to be revealed. And one person
was out to make sure they never remembered…

---

# Save $1.00 off

## your purchase of any
## Harlequin® Forrester Square title
## on-sale August 2003 through July 2004

RETAILER: Harlequin Enterprises Ltd. will pay the face value of this coupon plus
10.25¢ if submitted by customer for this product only. Any other use constitutes fraud.
Coupon is nonassignable. Void if taxed, prohibited or restricted by law. Void if copied.
Consumer must pay any government taxes. Valid in Canada only. Nielson Clearing
House customers—mail to: Harlequin Enterprises Ltd., 661 Millidge Avenue, P.O. Box
639, Saint John, N.B. E2L 4A5. Non NCH retailer—for reimbursement submit coupons
and proof of sales directly to: Harlequin Enterprises Ltd., Retail Sales Dept., 225
Duncan Mill Rd., Don Mills, Ontario M3B 3K9, Canada.

Coupon expires July 30, 2004.
Redeemable at participating retail outlets in Canada only.
Limit one coupon per purchase.

52605231

---

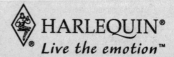

## HARLEQUIN®
### *Live the emotion*™

**Your opinion is important to us!** Please take a few moments to share your thoughts with us about your experiences with Harlequin and Silhouette books. Your comments will be very useful in ensuring that we deliver books you love to read.
*Please take a few minutes to complete the questionnaire, then send it to us at the address below.*

Send your completed questionnaires to:
**Harlequin/Silhouette Reader Survey, P.O. Box 9046, Buffalo, NY 14269-9046**

1. As you may know, there are many different lines under the Harlequin and Silhouette brands. Each of the lines is listed below. Please check the box that most represents your reading habit for each line.

| Line | Currently read this line | Do not read this line | Not sure if I read this line |
|---|---|---|---|
| Harlequin American Romance | ❏ | ❏ | ❏ |
| Harlequin Duets | ❏ | ❏ | ❏ |
| Harlequin Romance | ❏ | ❏ | ❏ |
| Harlequin Historicals | ❏ | ❏ | ❏ |
| Harlequin Superromance | ❏ | ❏ | ❏ |
| Harlequin Intrigue | ❏ | ❏ | ❏ |
| Harlequin Presents | ❏ | ❏ | ❏ |
| Harlequin Temptation | ❏ | ❏ | ❏ |
| Harlequin Blaze | ❏ | ❏ | ❏ |
| Silhouette Special Edition | ❏ | ❏ | ❏ |
| Silhouette Romance | ❏ | ❏ | ❏ |
| Silhouette Intimate Moments | ❏ | ❏ | ❏ |
| Silhouette Desire | ❏ | ❏ | ❏ |

2. Which of the following best describes why you bought *this book?* One answer only, please.

| | | | |
|---|---|---|---|
| the picture on the cover | ❏ | the title | ❏ |
| the author | ❏ | the line is one I read often | ❏ |
| part of a miniseries | ❏ | saw an ad in another book | ❏ |
| saw an ad in a magazine/newsletter | ❏ | a friend told me about it | ❏ |
| I borrowed/was given this book | ❏ | other: _____ | ❏ |

3. Where did you buy *this book?* One answer only, please.

| | | | |
|---|---|---|---|
| at Barnes & Noble | ❏ | at a grocery store | ❏ |
| at Waldenbooks | ❏ | at a drugstore | ❏ |
| at Borders | ❏ | on eHarlequin.com Web site | ❏ |
| at another bookstore | ❏ | from another Web site | ❏ |
| at Wal-Mart | ❏ | Harlequin/Silhouette Reader | ❏ |
| at Target | ❏ | Service/through the mail | |
| at Kmart | ❏ | used books from anywhere | ❏ |
| at another department store or mass merchandiser | ❏ | I borrowed/was given this book | ❏ |

4. On average, how many Harlequin and Silhouette books do you buy at one time?

| | |
|---|---|
| I buy _____ books at one time | ❏ |
| I rarely buy a book | ❏ |

MRQ403HAR-1A

5. How many times per month do you shop for any *Harlequin and/or Silhouette* books?
One answer only, please.

| | | | |
|---|---|---|---|
| 1 or more times a week | ❏ | a few times per year | ❏ |
| 1 to 3 times per month | ❏ | less often than once a year | ❏ |
| 1 to 2 times every 3 months | ❏ | never | ❏ |

6. When you think of your ideal heroine, which *one* statement describes her the best?
One answer only, please.

| | | | |
|---|---|---|---|
| She's a woman who is strong-willed | ❏ | She's a desirable woman | ❏ |
| She's a woman who is needed by others | ❏ | She's a powerful woman | ❏ |
| She's a woman who is taken care of | ❏ | She's a passionate woman | ❏ |
| She's an adventurous woman | ❏ | She's a sensitive woman | ❏ |

7. The following statements describe types or genres of books that you may be
interested in reading. Pick *up to 2 types* of books that you are most interested in.

| | |
|---|---|
| I like to read about truly romantic relationships | ❏ |
| I like to read stories that are sexy romances | ❏ |
| I like to read romantic comedies | ❏ |
| I like to read a romantic mystery/suspense | ❏ |
| I like to read about romantic adventures | ❏ |
| I like to read romance stories that involve family | ❏ |
| I like to read about a romance in times or places that I have never seen | ❏ |
| Other: _____ | ❏ |

*The following questions help us to group your answers with those readers who are
similar to you. Your answers will remain confidential.*

8. Please record your year of birth below.

19 ____

9. What is your marital status?

single ❏     married ❏     common-law ❏     widowed ❏
divorced/separated ❏

10. Do you have children 18 years of age or younger currently living at home?

yes ❏     no ❏

11. Which of the following best describes your employment status?

employed full-time or part-time ❏     homemaker ❏     student ❏
retired ❏     unemployed ❏

12. Do you have access to the Internet from either home or work?

yes ❏     no ❏

13. Have you ever visited eHarlequin.com?

yes ❏     no ❏

14. What state do you live in?

_____

15. Are you a member of Harlequin/Silhouette Reader Service?

yes ❏     Account # _____     no ❏     MRQ403HAR-1B

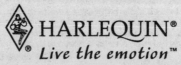